Finding

Famous

I hope you enjoy my story-

Alexis Anicque

Alexis Anicque
author
2-6-21

Contents:

ACKNOWLEDGEMENTS

There are no words to express how grateful I am to my beautiful niece Tiffany Hubbard for her love and support. I was fortunate to have her and her lovely friends Jess and Trevor to give me a quiet place of solace to finish this story. Tiffany is an amazing sounding board. I was surrounded by a lot of lovely pups and great friends.

Thank you Tiff, Jess, and Trevor. I am fortunate to have a friend like Tammy Petry, her constant encouragement gave me drive and confidence. She has been my greatest ally when doubt crept in.

Thank you, my beautiful friends.

PROLOGUE

A glimpse of movement in her peripheral vision froze Famous in her tracks. Something was moving toward her, she didn't dare move. The sound was coming closer. Famous was backing up to a tree slowly, so as to not make a sound. She was holding her breath for fear of the noise. Hoping against all hopes that whatever it was would turn and go in another direction. The brush was so thick she couldn't see a thing, but she could hear it coming for her. Her heart was pounding she wanted to run or scream or both.

Every terrifying second seemed like an hour. Maybe there was a pack of wolves surrounding her. She tried to imagine a fuzzy bunny or a harmless squirrel. She had backed herself up to a tree and crouched down low wanting to make herself invisible. The noises, the branches moving, was nearly more than she could handle. Tears began to stream down her face.

Her mothers' voice kept running through her head saying "There is not a monster in your closet Famous, I promise monsters have rules too and they aren't allowed in little girls' closets."

Famous would say, "Then they are under my bed mommy please let me sleep with you."

"They aren't allowed there either."

Famous would say, "What about behind my curtains" It's funny to think that she never denied the existence of monsters.

CHAPTER ONE

THE GREAT SADNESS

"Yes, my name is Famous," she answered for the thousandth time. Her mother had always said she would be, famous that is. She knew it from the day she had found her. Believing she had some type of psychic ability, she would tell Famous that it was just a matter of time. But famous, she was not. In fact nothing even remotely famous had ever happened in her life.

She lived in a small fishing village a couple of hours north of New York City. A small town with the population of roughly five hundred. Life there, to her, was boring and mundane. But it was her normal, wake up get dressed, and go to work. Her days off, were much like her days at work which consisted of reading or writing a book.

Famous worked for the local library where she had worked since she was fifteen years old. It was actually the only job she had ever had. It started out as a credit for high school. Then volunteering after school and summers, until she was hired on as paid summer help. Finally after high school she has hired on full time. She had imagined that she would work there forever. Her mother had been the dreamer. The one who had all of the hopes for her future.

Famous loved the library, she lived through the pages of other people's stories. She began reading every title, no matter what it was. She read poetry, cooking, romance, even auto mechanics. The list was endless, she had read nearly every book in the young adult section. Sometimes her imagination would run wild like she was on the adventure right along with the characters. Reading was her first passion, but writing was a close second. Writing a novel every couple of months that she never intended to get published. Her mother used to say, "Famous it's your destiny, one day you'll be a famous author on the best seller's list."

Famous would simply say, "I don't write to be famous."

She dreamt of finding love under a moonlit sky, climbing through a rain forest, or hiding in an ice cave like the stories her mother would tell. Famous once asked "how could she have possibly thought up all these crazy stories."

Her mother simply said "It took me many great adventures to find you Famous. One day you will take such an adventure." But she said nothing more on the subject until it neared her death. "Famous", she said, "You must follow my adventures, the journey I took to find you Famous. You must take this journey it is waiting for you. Go to the house, it's there that I have left you the path to follow." She took a deep breath, "I Love you, Famous." Her final words and she was gone. Famous was heartbroken, so much so that she couldn't think of what her mother was saying to her.

Her mother died in the summer after her 21st birthday. Famous called it the time of her greatest sadness. Her mother had always been like magic to Famous. You could see her, you couldn't explain her, and she would entrance you. Famous often thought of her mother. She missed her more than ever, but felt blessed for the memories she had had with the woman who she had believed was the most amazing and mystical person in the entire world that ever existed. Each novel Famous had written had come from the stories her mother had told her throughout the years of her life.

Nearly seven years had passed, she still had not thought of what her mother had said on her deathbed. One night in a dream she heard her mother's dying words. "I have left you the path to follow." Her mother had come to her several times in dreams before, but in this particular dream she spoke with such urgency. Famous woke, feeling certain that her mother was there with her.

It was to her fortune Famous was able to continue to live in the house. She had always thought the house was charming. More like a cottage than a house. Decorated with photos of her mother, before and after finding Famous. There were books on shelves and a few candles, but that was it. Charming and quaint. There was a studio apartment above the garage that had a kitchenette and bathroom. They had rented it out over the years. Which is how, Famous figured, her mother had paid the note off years before. It was also how Famous was paying the taxes every year since. The cottage had been her saving grace.

Her room had been up in the loft where she could peer down into the living area. Her mother's room had a door behind the base of the stairs. She couldn't bear to go into her mother's room. But she was certain that is where mother must have left the path she spoke of. After only a couple of months had passed, Famous went in her mother's room. She could smell her mother's perfume, the sweet heavenly scent like she was still there. Famous lied on her bed and cried, she left the room, closed the door, and had not opened it since.

Exactly seven years after her death, Famous had finally decided it was time. She opened the door very slowly. Looking in she could visualize her mother laughing and saying I have another story Famous, come sit on the bed with me. Those were the best times in her life. Thinking how disappointed she might be that she had done nothing in the past seven years. A prison term life sentence in some countries.

It was dark so Famous pulled open the curtains. The room was filled with dust and cob webs. It was time, actually beyond time to fill this room with life again. Maybe she could find a roommate, it was hard to picture anyone else living in this space besides her mother. It was and would always be her mother's room.

The door creaked as she opened the closet, she saw her clothes and could picture her in every item as she removed them from the hangers. The room wasn't as sad as it had been before. Carefully she packed the clothes in boxes except those she chose to keep. The ones that reminded her of her the most or ones Famous thought she might wear. The shoes were too large for Famous so she packed them all away, thinking that a shelter would be a nice place to take them and may help someone. Her mother would be happy that her things were doing good rather than not being used.

There wasn't a lot there, just two boxes in the top of the closet. Surely she was missing something. Pulling down the first box and examining the contents. Some train tickets, a map, a necklace piece of some kind, and a napkin from some place in Ireland. Souvenirs, she guessed. A bunch of other miscellaneous items. The second box was full of her journals. She opened several looking at the dates. Finding the one for the year she must have begun her journey to find Famous. She began to read.

'She came to me in a dream, Famous, a baby looking for a mother. The next day I began my quest for finding Famous.'

There was a small piece of paper like a sticky note added, 'If you are reading this Famous then I am gone. Stop reading and pack your bags, it is time for your adventure to begin. There are clues in the box next to the box of journals.

She stared at the journal, not knowing what to do. This was just like her, Famous thought, drop everything and go now. She couldn't possibly just pack her bags and leave tomorrow the way her mother had all those years before. Yet, if she continued to read it was showing such disrespect to the memory of her mother. Her mother would have had to know that for Famous it would be necessary to get things in order. That would not be the way her mother would think though.

Famous didn't know what to pack, she didn't dare read ahead in the journal. Famous sat at the edge of the bed staring at the page in the journal. She had no idea what would happen next. The journal snapped closed and startled her. She was certain that she had imagined the whole thing. The same little note was sitting right on top! She read it over and over. Logic told Famous to read on in the journal, but she would not even attempt to open it.

Unlike her mother, she was scared to just pack her bags and run out the door. This was a fear she would soon have overcome. Running to the loft, she began to pull out clothes. Wondering what to take, how much should she take, if only her mother had said more than just 'pack your bag' as if she would know what she needed for the journey? Famous was thinking, where am I going? She knew her mother well enough to know that she would say 'pack only what you can easily carry.' She would often say the same of burdens and stress.

Famous was certain that her mother had learned this freedom from her mother. She could only imagine, but Famous knew her mother's name was as odd as her own. Dar Alegria, roughly meaning give joy in Spanish, although Famous didn't remember her grandmother she had imagined her many times from the stories her mother had told.

Hastily she packed a backpack, thinking she would just have to make due. Sending an email to the librarian saying she would be taking some time off to do some traveling and she was sincerely sorry it was so last minute.

CHAPTER TWO

WHERE AM I GOING

The beginning of the second page of the journal her mother wrote,

"I did not know where I was going, only that I was going. I could hear life beckoning me to go. I immediately packed and went to the train station."

A second note: Famous you must go to the train station travel north into Canada and once you're on the train read the next few pages you will know when to stop.

"I'll know when to stop, how? How will I know when to stop?" She was staring up as if talking to the ceiling.

Again the journal snapped closed. She jumped and realized she hadn't imagined it at all. Famous remembered the train tickets in the box of souvenirs. She emptied the contents into her backpack and would look at them when she got to the train station.

The journey began just like that, Famous left her little cottage. The place of her childhood, the safety of her home to the unknown. The train station was a short walk,

9

though for Famous it was a great distance of uncertainty. She had hours to wait and had even thought about walking home to wait. But wasn't certain she would have the courage to leave the cottage a second time. As she sat in the station she longed to read on in the journal, but could hear her mother saying, 'be patient Famous everything happens as it should and in the time it should happen. You mustn't rush destiny.'

She felt the journals in her bag and could feel her mother there with her, like she had not felt in years. Famous felt alive again, a part of her had died the day her mother passed. Sitting there she wondered if that is when her mother had come to find her, when her own mother had passed. She had so many questions.

The train station was small with very few people. Famous found only one train going north to Canada, she didn't even know where she was to go, just north. Perhaps the old ticket stub her mom had left will be the clue. Stepping on the platform she could feel herself being pushed toward the train. Glancing back, thinking she could still turn back and go home. She stepped up on the train and found a seat in the first car. As the train left the station she opened the journal and began to read.

"My journey began in a small train station today, I could hear it calling me. I left my home and traveled on the very first train out which led me to a nomad's cottage in the mountains of Canada. I should say he was a wizard, of sorts." (There was a small note saying she must find the wizard who holds a message for Famous.)

Famous pondered this message, what it must say, a message, she can only guess from her mother.

"I watched as the train journeyed north. I would see the people in the towns and imagine what they must be doing. Living their lives, did they have a family, who were they and how did they spend their time? I had my mother who was an amazing mother, I hope when I find my child I will be as well."

This made Famous smile and feel so warm and connected to her knowing that she was the most amazing mother ever.

"It was raining and in the dark of the night when I knew it was my stop. I was just going in the direction of my calling. I walked and walked through the forest. I heard the cry of animals and the call of an owl. I did not feel fear as I knew this was the journey I must take to find my little one. Hours had gone by and I was sure I was lost walking in the cold of night, it began to rain.

I took shelter and the wizard, Jeremiah, found me huddled under a tree escaping the rain. He called my name, although I had not met him before. Picking me up and carrying me to his cottage and placing me by the fire."

He said, "Dear little Dar, I have been waiting for you. What has taken you so long?"

Famous couldn't believe what she was reading, how is such a thing even possible?

"I slept by the warmth of the fire for hours. My dreams were so vivid of a girl lost looking for answers that only I could give. I imagined her to be petite with long flowing strawberry blonde hair. She called me mother, I knew it was a dream or a vision of what was to come. When I awoke, I was confused by where I was.

Jeremiah had prepared a meal for me. He was a very little, chubby, old man. I asked how he knew my name, but he pretended he didn't know what I was talking about. He said in the coming days when I was completely rested we would take a journey to the waterfall. This journey would take time, but there were answers for me in the waterfall.

I wasn't clear on who he was, or what he was talking about, but I felt like I was destined to follow him." (another small note: and you will as well, Famous)

Famous stared out the window, it was turning dusk. She wasn't sure where she was going when the train stopped. So far, there had been no clue, really, just a cottage in the mountains lived in by a wizard. She giggled, when she thought about that. It's not like you can just ask directions, "Hey, can you tell me how to get to the wizards cottage?" That kind of question might get someone put in a hospital. She would just have to continue reading.

Her mother was always talking about her adventures and Famous believed every word. It was only now on this train when she had a sudden thought, what if she had made it all up? Just fun and amazing stories you tell a child. That wouldn't explain the journal, but Famous could be taking a journey to a pretend place. A cottage in the forest sounded believable enough, but a wizard. Famous pushed these thoughts out of her head.

Turning the page there was a map to the cottage from the stop she was to get off at with a note, not to read further until she reached the cottage. The journal snapped closed again, Famous wasn't sure she would ever understand or get used to that.

Famous drifted off to sleep, she dreamt of her mother and the wizard making the long journey to the waterfall.

CHAPTER THREE

MONSTERS HAVE RULES

Famous slept for hours and she was awakened by the conductor asking for her ticket. She asked about the stop and he said she had missed that stop. By how far she wasn't clear. The train stopped at the next station and put her off. Famous was thinking it is in the dark of the night just as my mother had traveled, but unlike her mother she was afraid. Because she had missed her stop, she was already lost before even leaving the station. Trying to be positive she thought at least it isn't raining. The station was dark and there was no one in sight, the challenge was she had absolutely no clue where she was, nor where she was going.

She had a destination, almost a laughable destination, a wizards' cottage in the forest. Famous chuckled at the thought. She remembered stories she had read through the years in the library about wizards and mystical adventures like this, but never in a million years did she believe she would be right in the middle of such a fairy tale. A grand adventure she would say after she read such a novel.

Famous took a look at the map in the journal, but it was an odd map. One, she was sure her mother had drawn along the way. There were smudges where she was sure it must have been from drops of rain. Odd pictures of trees, rocks, or a fork in a path. She ran her fingers across the words and imagined her mother under a tree trying to draw this map. Probably to help find her way back to the train, if she couldn't figure out what she was looking for.

Famous thought of her mother wandering through the forest unsure of her destination. She thought it was different for her and yet the same. She didn't know why she was taking this journey but knew kind of where she was going, the places her mother had gone. Her mother didn't know where she was going, but she knew why.

It was at that moment for her, something happened as she was visioning her mother unafraid, listening to the sounds of animals, and trying to stay dry in a cold dark forest. She could feel her, telling Famous, "don't worry, my dear little one I will find you." Suddenly she felt the urge to begin walking being guided by just a feeling. Famous would later describe in her own journal as a magical, mystical feeling. She took a paper and began her own map as she walked a pathway into the dark forest.

Famous thought of the things that were different for her, a phone with GPS that doubles as a flashlight, but she had to conserve the battery. Charging it would be a challenge. The moon was bright and assisted her when there was a clearing. She used these times to draw her map and see if anything resembles her mother's map. She took her time carefully marking trees, large rocks, or distinguishing paths. The sounds of the night weren't nearly as terrifying as she had thought. Sometimes a crack of a branch or a call of a wolf would startle her and make her jump.

At one point she was thinking she had been walking in circles. Every tree looks the same she thought, but then she would see something unlike anything she had seen before. She knew she would have put it on her map, like a creek or a broken tree. Her fear, then lack of fear changed from minute to minute. Thinking why had she not waited until daylight? An owl called out in the darkness and Famous remembered that from her mother's journal. She sat with her phone looking at her map against her mother's. Famous was just so unsure of where her mother had begun her map all those years ago.

Certainly time had changed the appearances of her landmarks as well.

A glimpse of movement in her peripheral vision froze Famous in her tracks. Something was moving toward her, she didn't dare move. The sound was coming closer. Famous was backing up to a tree slowly, so as to not make a sound. She was holding her breath for fear of the noise. Hoping against all hopes that whatever it was would turn and go in another direction. The brush was so thick she couldn't see a thing, but she could hear it coming for her. Her heart was pounding she wanted to run or scream or both.

Every terrifying second seemed like an hour. Maybe there was a pack of wolves surrounding her. She tried to imagine a fuzzy bunny or a harmless squirrel. She had backed herself up to a tree and crouched down low wanting to make herself invisible. The noises, the branches moving, was nearly more than she could handle. Tears began to stream down her face.

Her mothers' voice kept running through her head saying "There is not a monster in your closet Famous, I promise monsters have rules too and they aren't allowed in little girls' closets."

Famous would say, "Then they are under my bed mommy please let me sleep with you."

"They aren't allowed there either."

Famous would say, "What about behind my curtains" It's funny to think that she never denied the existence of monsters. Famous had never considered that until right this moment. Now all she could think of is what about here in the forest, are they allowed here in the forest? She knew it was silly, but couldn't stop the thoughts. Stories would usually calm her in a stressful situation. Not that she had many stressful situations in her life other than losing her mother. The time of great sadness was very stressful.

The thought of climbing the tree had crossed her mind. Although, with some creatures, she would be just a treed animal for the taking. The noise quieted and she felt a calm until a branch moved again and she nearly jumped out of her skin. What can it be? It is toying with her, paralyzing her with fear, easy prey. She inched around the tree in the opposite direction. Hugging her legs she placed her head on her knees, closed her eyes and waited, for what she didn't know.

CHAPTER FOUR

LIGHTENING BUGS TO FRESH BAKED BREAD

It seemed as if time were standing still while her mind was filled with visions of bears and beasts in the night. Why had she not waited for the light of day? It is a quest, she thought, she must take. Opening her eyes she saw the lights, the most amazing lights of the lightening bugs. She arose feeling unafraid, a feeling of peace and warmth overcame her as she walked toward the lights. As if they were guiding her, showing the way to the place she needed to go. In the distance she could hear the rustling of the bushes, but it was as if she were wearing a shield.

It is amazing how aware you become of life and everything in it. Even the wind had a different sound in the dark. A trickle in the distance of running water, it must be a creek or a river. Maybe it led to this waterfall she was supposed to find. The waterfall wasn't supposed to be her first destination. Perhaps her journey will not take her to the cottage in the woods. Lightening bugs fluttered all around her which gave her joy and the strength to walk on.

The sun will come soon, Famous told herself over and over. Even though she had no idea of the time, it comforted her. Walking aware of the absolute absence of color here in the dark. When the sun is up the rainbow of colors will come alive. The green trees, the blue sky, the orange and pink flowers. The possibility of red berries on bushes. She was amazed at how her senses were heightened by the darkness.

The cracking sound of a branch, crunching leaves, she knew she must be being followed. A monster behind her in the darkness or a case of an over active imagination. She could hide until the morning, but she pushed on. As if the wind were a hand gently nudging her forward. Careful to make notes that she was unsure would matter in the light of day. Everything looks different in the daylight.

She could hear the water rushing louder now, still aware of the sounds behind her. Was she being taunted or protected alone in the forest, but she wasn't alone. She could feel she wasn't alone, she didn't know what or who was there in the blackness following her footsteps.

Her heart was beating so hard in her chest. Her pace quickened toward the sound of the water. It was funny to her how sound is amplified in the dark as well. Famous could hear the river, it sounded so close and yet she had no idea how far it could be.

She was feeling so sleepy, so very sleepy. A rest might be good for her. Just lie down and take a nap she kept telling herself. Of course a voice in her head said she would be just a sitting duck for what lurked behind her in the darkness. Surely, there must be a place where she could feel safe. If even for only a little while. Some bushes that she could nestle in or a place where she could rest her head. Coming to a cove, Famous had found the river. Unsure of whether to go upstream or downstream she looked for a place to sleep. She lied down in a field near a large tree. Still very aware of the sounds of the night as she drifted off to the land where dreams come from.

She could see her mother smiling telling the story about falling in the ice cave. She was saved by a monk, had he not come along, she surely would have died. She would regale Famous with stories like this as they baked cakes and bread. Famous could smell the bread, the heavenly sent of baking bread. The smell seemed so real. Her eyes started to flutter, it was the beginning of the day. When, as her mother would say, everything and anything is possible. Each day is a new beginning, a chance to start anew. She kept going back to the smell of baking bread, suddenly certain she could smell bread baking. It was unmistakably, that heavenly scent of baking bread.

CHAPTER FIVE

THE WIZARD OF SORTS

An aroma of flowers and bread baking filled her nose. The dim light from the rising sun and again baking bread. Famous was reaching to find a snack in her pack. She thought, she must just be hungry from a dream of her mother's bread, but the smell was so strong. Sitting up, she became very aware that she was no longer dreaming. Yet she could still smell bread baking. Now her stomach was growling.

Something was coming, she could hear the footsteps. It was still dim, she couldn't see through the field of flowers, bright purple flowers. On any other day she would gaze in amazement at those beautiful flowers. But the fear of something coming closer and closer distracted her from such amazement. Maybe it had been waiting for the sun, or just enough light to see its prey. Glancing around for a stick or rock, anything she could protect herself with. There was nothing but flowers.

Closer and closer, the steps were coming, she sunk down as low as she could. Maybe it would pass by her not knowing she was there. Crouching lower and lower, nearly laying on the soft, damp earth.

"Famous, I presume?" The voice startled her so badly she thought she may have a heart attack. "You must be hungry child." He was chubby with rosy red cheeks and a stubby nose. Her eyes widened with wonder, the wizard, she thought. He's real, somewhere in her mind she had not believed there really was a wizard. Yet here he stood. Famous nodded as she reached for his outstretched hand.

He wasn't a dwarf, but nearly as small. His smile radiated comfort and love. "Hello," she stuttered and managed a confused smile.

"Come child, come to the safety of my cottage. You mustn't be left here any longer." He glanced back into the darkness, at what, Famous didn't know and was sure she didn't want to know. He took her hand rushing her down the riverside. Looking back on several occasions. Again Famous could hear the crunching of leaves and cracking of twigs behind her, but now she was not alone.

"What is it?" She whispered, "What is there in the darkness?"

"It's nothing to worry about now." His voice was reassuring, but Famous didn't feel reassured. Of course if something had been there, why had it not come for her while she was sleeping? "We will talk over breakfast, now come along, my dear."

The rainbow of colors were beginning to get brighter. The smell of baking bread even stronger, smoke from a chimney she imagined but could not yet see. She could see a path in the distance leading to an archway made from bushes, an opening where the sun was shining brightly. He had slowed to a casual pace as they passed through the arch, a cobble stone pathway to a cottage so quaint, it reminded her of the cottage of the seven dwarves. A cozy little cottage nestled in the woods with a stone face and a smoking chimney.

She walked in to see a lovely little wood stove with fresh baked bread in a basket on the table. The light streamed in from little windows. He ushered her to the chair and poured some tea. "How is your mother?" He asked, but she knew that he had known the answer to his question. She could tell by the tone of sadness in his voice.

"I think you know the answer."

"Yes sadly, I do. I had so hoped I was wrong." He busied himself cutting the bread adding an icing top and placing a plate in front of her. Famous took a bite, she tasted orange, and cinnamon. A combination she hadn't imagined before. It was sweet, warm, and gooey. Simply the most delicious bread she had ever had. Famous wondered if that would delight or sadden her mother. Maybe both as she loved Famous so and would want her to enjoy it, yet she had so much pride in her baking abilities.

"How did you know it was me and that I was there in the field?" She looked at him with curiosity in her eyes as she was sure her mother had so many years before. He said nothing as if the question hadn't been asked. Just going about getting another slice of bread and pouring more tea. "What was it that was following me?" Again he said nothing.

Finally turning to her with a big smile he asked, "Do you know why you are here, Famous?"

"I think so," she stuttered "I'm following the journey to where my mom found me."

He nodded, "Do you think that is the only reason for your journey?"

"I, well I guess I am not totally sure," she shrugged. "Maybe I have to learn something that would be like my mother sending me on a quest for knowledge." She saw something move in the corner of the next room. Turning her head to look, there was nothing there. Glancing in the other room and thinking how it looked so cozy. She got up and walked away from the table, seeing a little fireplace with big overstuffed pillows, kind of like small pillow mattresses.

"Your mother slept there," he pointed at the one near the fireplace, "On the night I found her in the rain. She was cold, she laid there to warm herself and sleep took her quickly. What a lovely, lovely creature she was." He smiled fondly at the memory. Famous could see her sleeping there in her mind.

Again she thought she saw movement and turned to see nothing. How curious, she thought, maybe she was just tired or even still asleep and only dreaming. "The bread was so delicious. I've never had bread like that. My mother and I baked together often, nearly every day and it was always wonderful. I think that yours was the best bread that I have ever tasted."

"When you live alone in the forest, you have time to be creative and even can learn to master skills. Your mother and I baked together, it gives me great joy to hear that she continued to bake."

"We baked together and she told me stories, fairy tales, well I thought they were, but now I'm just not sure. I don't know what to believe or even to think. Maybe this isn't really happening. Oh I just... never mind I'm sounding silly I suppose."

"Do you wish it to be just a dream? Look deep within your heart Famous. You've come a long way in just a short time. It has been only a day in your journey. What will you believe in a week? What will have changed in you?" He placed his arm around her shoulders in what she believed would be a fatherly manner and gave her a little squeeze.

She did want to know where she had come from, who was her father. If her mother had found her who was her biological mother and what happened to her? How had she gotten so lucky to have been found by Dar Alegria. Named so appropriately because she did give joy to anything and everyone she touched. "I want to know everything and experience it all, when do we leave?"

He patted her on the back, "You will know as time allows you to know." He walked to the kitchen to clear the dishes from the table. She had no idea what he meant, but she was getting used to that feeling.

CHAPTER SIX

PATIENCE

Famous had spent the day in the garden with Jeremiah, picking tomatoes, cucumbers, pulling onions, digging potatoes and other various fruits and vegetables. She had forgotten the last words she had read in the journal. When she thought of it she wanted to run in and read on, but there was no reason to hurry. It was a lovely day and Jeremiah was telling stories of her mother's visit.

She loved to listen to him talk about her. The magic of her trailed through his voice. There were so many questions she longed to ask, but Jeremiah avoided answering questions. He told stories and one must listen very carefully to find the answers within his tales. She was still very unclear on why her mother said he was a wizard, of sorts. Famous didn't really know what would make a person a wizard, magic she guessed, but Jeremiah seemed like just a regular old man. Although she had only been there half of a day nothing significant stood out that said the contrary.

They walked with pails to collect the water for the day from the nearby river. "I always collect enough for the evening even if it takes several trips. I never go to the river after dark." He sounded mysterious, but Famous knew it would be useless to ask why. "When we return, you and I can make lunch. Maybe we will talk about our journey to the waterfall."

"I'd like that, what is there at the waterfall?"

"You will see, patience will show you." His words reminded her of words her mother often said. Maybe this is where she learned them. A thought crossed her mind that possibly her mother wanted her to learn the things she had not yet taught her at an age when she would understand them. The same age her mother was when she had taken this journey. Perhaps her mother knew she would be unable to teach her. "You seem deep in thought Famous."

"I was just thinking about my mother, sometimes I analyze things to death. Your words reminded me of something she would say to me, that's all."

"Oh and what was that?"

"You know, just that things would happen when they were supposed to happen. The whole patience thing, I guess."

They made two trips carrying water back to the cottage. Famous prattled on about taking baked goods to shelters with her mom because they baked too much to eat. Regaling Jeremiah with wonderful stories of the childhood she had had. Sharing her work at the library and how many books she had read through the years. He listened with the grandest smile. Famous was sure that although he loved his simple life it gave him joy to have company.

Jeremiah prepared tomatoes stuffed with some type of fish and vegetables. So fresh and delicious, another meal she had never had that amazed her by the flavors. "Maybe we shall make another trip to the river, if we are lucky, we can enjoy a salmon for dinner. Although, I do have alternatives in the cellar if we are not lucky enough to catch a salmon. Your mother loved fishing, did she ever take you?" Famous nodded and said she would love to go. "We must clean up first then we will go." Just as it had been all of her life. You must clean up so you can start fresh, that thought made her smile. Come to think of it her mother was always about starting fresh or a new beginning. Moving on from the past. Another thing she is just now realizing. There are many lessons to be learned in life, but they must be learned when you are ready to learn them.

After collecting some handmade fishing poles from the cellar and digging worms from the garden they were off to the river. The sweet scent of lavender filled her senses. Reminding her of the bubble bath she had near her tub back home. Thinking of home she wondered if the librarian had emailed her back. She was certain she would have no service on her phone out here in the middle of the forest. Of course there wasn't electricity to plug her phone in either. She may as well not bother to turn the silly thing on at all. This is what life was like before technology. Not bad, but Famous did enjoy the internet.

Jeremiah put the worm on the hook for her, she said it was just too slimy and wriggled around too much. He said her mother was the same way, a silly girl, he supposed most girls are so silly. Picturing her mother, they had gone fishing, but they had real fishing poles and bought bait. A tug on her line brought her back to reality. She yanked the pole in hopes of setting the hook. It was fighting her, pulling and pulling. Famous didn't know what to do there wasn't a reel to reel it in. She was having a hard time just keeping hold of the make-shift pole. Jeremiah was laughing and realizing her struggles, he grabbed the pole and helped her yank the giant salmon from the water. They tumbled to the ground laughing as the fish flopped around in the grass.

"You caught more than enough for dinner, wow is that ever a grand fish." He put it in the pail. "That was quite exciting wasn't it?" Laughter filled the air, Famous could hardly wait to write about this in her own journal. She had again forgotten about her mother's journal. It had been such a wonderful day she would wait for the evening after writing about her day to read on in the journal.

CHAPTER SEVEN

A FURRY LITTLE CREATURE

Jeremiah cleaned and filleted the salmon while Famous cleaned potatoes and vegies for dinner. Her head was filled with the day and thoughts of her mother's journal. What surprises waited for her in the coming days. That led her to question how long this journey would take. Money was not an issue, she had saved most of her paychecks for all the years she worked. Her mother had left her a meager savings, but she had left so abruptly without much word, she feared people may get concerned. She had left a message for her tenant and an email to the librarian, but she knew she would have to contact the outside world in the next few days.

There was something moving across the floor that caught her eye in the other room. She walked around the corner to look, but there was nothing there. It seemed very curious and she knew there must be some kind of pet or maybe he had a mouse problem. She certainly didn't want to upset him by assuming anything.

She supposed she could investigate later.
Famous watched as Jeremiah prepared the
salmon. He was going to bake it with lemon,
butter, garlic, and herbs. "Where do you get
your butter from?"

"There is a farmer down the way that trades
with me for butter and cheese, occasionally
milk and cream, but I don't really use them as
often."

"Oh and what do you trade with him?"

"It varies," he was mysterious in his tone
and offered no more information. "Maybe you
can set the table, dinner won't be too much
longer."

"Yes, of course, oh and thank you. It seems
I have forgotten my manners."

"For what?"

"Finding me, feeding me, and well just
everything."

He smiled, "You are welcome, and you are
also always welcome as your mother was."
Jeremiah helped to set things on the table.
"Well it looks as if we will eat like royalty."
Letting out a big snort as he laughed made
Famous giggle.

Dinner was succulent, she ate until she
could just eat no more. After dinner they sat by
the fire and chatted about the trip to the
waterfall. He was very cryptic and non-

committal about the whole thing. They would leave when she was ready. There were dangers, it would take some time, saying a lot without saying anything. "You said my mother was always welcome did my mother come back here?"

"Your journey is her story and in a way yours as well, I shall let you take that journey and you will know." Answers without answers she thought. She could attempt to read into what he had said or ask a million more questions, but Famous knew that she would have the same information as when she had started asking.

Jeremiah had finally turned in for the night. Famous took out her journal and her mother's as well. She wrote about the day before and today making it to be a beginning of her grand adventure. She even added her map from the previous night. It had been quite an exciting two days she thought. She wondered if her mother thought the same as she was here by the fire.

Snuggling down on the cushion her mother had snuggled on years before her. Famous opened her mother's journal that she, was too excited for words, to read. She had had amazing restraint waiting the whole day. Many times through the day she had wanted to run in and grab it from her pack to read on. She felt she would be being rude to her lovely host if she had. There was a small note at the top of the page, *"Famous I am glad you made it to the cottage, I love you so much."* The words brought tears to her eyes as she read them several times. She continued on to read what she had written so many years before.

"I stayed here with Jeremiah for several days. We baked, fished, worked in the garden, and I even played with the furry creatures that roamed the house. So sweet and cuddly, their species is still yet undetermined. I am getting ahead of myself, I remember the night the creatures arrived, more about that later."

Famous glanced around the small quaint room, shadows danced on the walls from the fire, but she saw no furry creatures. Curious she thought, maybe she had seen something move after all.

"The meals Jeremiah prepared were as if I had stepped into a five star restaurant. I also learned many things from him about baking. I had no idea what brought me to this little cottage, but it was a place I knew I needed to be. Late one evening I heard noises from the cellar, I tiptoed to the door and as I opened it a blue glow arose from the depths of the stairs. I could see the farmer and Jeremiah's shadows were upon the stairwell as I crept down the stairs. I was trying to be

as quiet as a mouse. It's hard to put into words what I saw."

A noise jolted Famous and she glanced around the room. She saw nothing, setting her mother's journal down she arose to investigate. She looked behind the curio cabinet, the other cushions about the room, she looked in every nook and cranny, but nothing. It gets more and more curious she thought. Shaking her head she returned to her cozy little area and began to read. It was so late and her eyes were so sleepy she managed only a few more words before she had fallen off to sleep.

Dreams of her mother with cuddly little bunnies surrounded by a bright blue light. She could see she was in the cottage and see a waterfall just outside the windows. There was a rainbow and beautiful trees surrounded by flowers of all different colors. She could nearly smell the sweet floral scent. The dream was so vivid and colorful. She could hear her mother singing and talking softly to the bunnies or was it to her. She tried to listen, but it was so muffled. She could hear her say her name, "Famous, my sweet Famous." It all seemed so real.

Suddenly something ran across her and then back, and landed on her stomach, she sat up and almost screamed. She was face to face with a furry little creature. Staring eye to eye, but neither of them moved. Famous was thinking, what do I do now? Should I yell for Jeremiah, or... her mind raced as the creature got closer and closer to her face. Famous leaned back she was nearly laying down flat with nowhere to go. The little fur ball began rubbing it's head on her cheek. It curled up next to her and went to sleep. Famous thought its behavior reminded her of a cat, it was definitely not a cat, she thought. Deciding to lie down and accept the cuddly little thing when she felt another curl up next to her as well. Giving the soft ball of fur a pat she drifted off back to sleep.

CHAPTER EIGHT

THE INCIDENT

There is nothing better than waking up to the smell of bacon cooking. Famous opened her eyes only to see the furry little critters were gone. She had wondered if she had imagined them, but read about them in her mother's journal. Her mother had played with them and cuddled them. Then she was reminded she had not read as much as she had hoped. The day had tired her and she drifted off before she had the chance and at such an interesting part.

Jeremiah called her to come for breakfast, she had so many questions. She was sure he wouldn't answer them, even still she was going to ask about the critters. She offered to help, however everything was ready. Famous apologized that she wasn't awake in time to help. Jeremiah said sleep was important and not to worry, he was overjoyed at having someone to cook for besides himself. She sat at the table he placed the plate in front of her. Heavenly was the only word that came to mind. Her mother would fix big breakfasts like this on Sundays. Eggs, bacon, special hash browns, and cinnamon toast.

"Jeremiah?"

"Hmm?"

"There were some little animals and well I was wondering?"

"Oh, don't you worry about them they won't hurt you."

"Yes I know they are quite lovable but what are they?"

"Oh, I have recently learned they are related to the long-eared jerboa, at least I think, anyway, part of the rodent family. Not really indigenous to this area, but I conjured them up by mere accident one evening." Famous thought that was a strange way to say something, conjured, what an odd choice of words. He continued on "Didn't your mother include the incident in her journal?"

"I fell asleep while reading last night so maybe it shall be in my reading today."

"Oh, that won't do, you're behind schedule, Famous."

"I... I...I'm sorry I wasn't aware there was a schedule."

"Oh no never mind, let's just eat our breakfast." His smile was bright and he had a twinkle in his eye. She imagined him to be what a grandpa would be like or maybe even Santa

41

Clause, well if there was such a thing, of course. "We won't tire out so much today you can just relax and read. We have to get back on track tomorrow we begin our journey to the waterfall."

After cleaning the breakfast dishes, Famous went to her comfy little cushion, picked up her mother's journal, and began to read where she had left off.

"It's hard to put into words what I saw. Jeremiah was reading from a book while the farmer was holding a small chick. There was an unexplained glow surrounding them, as Jeremiah began sprinkling something in the air and I was mesmerized by sparks and smoke. I started stretching forward so I could see better then I slipped on the stair and fell with a thud which startled Jeremiah. Suddenly everything went dark. When he lit the candle and ran to my side to check on me I saw them, the three little creatures. They were so cute and had ears as long as their whole body. Jeremiah scooped them up, placed them in my hands and sent me upstairs.

I waited and waited for them to come up the stairs, but fell asleep with my new little friends nuzzled in my neck."

A few hours passed as Famous read about the following days in the journal, they were normal days very much like her first day there. She was very detailed and quite specific about getting water, fishing, and etcetera. Nothing significant stood out and nothing was mentioned about the night in the cellar. On the third day after the cellar incident, as it was called by Jeremiah, they began their journey to the waterfall.

"Jeremiah said I needed to visit the waterfall and we would be leaving this morning. I gathered my things while he packed some food and water. He was singing a song and happy as could be. He said we would travel by day and would need to find a safe place to sleep at night. It was somewhat ominous the way he said it, but I was eager to go. I had become somewhat restless over the past couple of days not knowing truly why I was here. We set out early in the morning just after dawn, starting by the river and walking upstream. The forest was particularly beautiful on this morning. I remember thinking how green the trees were and how bright the flowers looked."

On the bottom of this page was a small note to Famous saying not to turn the page until after she reached the waterfall. Her mother said she wanted her journey to be her own and not changed by the following pages. Famous closed the journal and sighed. She was surprised that it didn't snap closed this time. She half-heartedly thought about continuing to read, when Jeremiah appeared in the doorway. "Grand you're all caught up." She wondered how he had known but left it alone. "Now we will begin our day."

Jeremiah grabbed some pails and motioned Famous to follow him. He said they would be preparing things for their journey. Baking some bread, catching and cooking some fish, and such. Famous was excited about going to the waterfall, of course, she was also wondering why it was such a big deal to see this particular waterfall as she was quite certain there were many waterfalls.

The day was filled with baking and cooking. Gathering fruit and vegetables. Famous was beginning to wonder how long this journey would take considering the amount of food they were taking. Jeremiah said, "It was better to be safe than sorry. Too much food is always better than not enough." After it was all packed, Famous thought they would never be able to carry it all. Jeremiah simply said a few words and the pack was as small as a coin purse. "There" he announced, "that will do us quite nicely."

Famous was staring in amazement, "If you can do that, why can't you just make food appear?"

"Don't be silly Famous, those are two completely different tasks. I am merely just minimizing our load, besides wouldn't that be quite lazy? Wouldn't it make life boring if you could or would just make anything you want appear?" He looked at her with raised eyebrows.

"Yes, I suppose but…"

He interrupted her, "half of life's experiences are based on the work that we must do to experience them. Did you enjoy baking and fishing today?"

She smiled thinking of all the funny stories he told of her mother with flour in her hair. Falling into the river because the fish was so big it pulled her in instead of her mother pulling it out of the water. They had laughed and talked of books Famous had read, it had been a lovely day. She nodded and said she did very much enjoy the day.

"Well if I made the food appear, none of that would have happened." He said it in a quite matter of fact way. She realized that this was probably something her mother had learned from Jeremiah as well. Famous was exhausted, after dinner, she laid down and fell fast asleep. Jeremiah blew out the candles and set off to bed, for he knew the following day would be a long one.

CHAPTER NINE

PERHAPS I WAS STILL DREAMING

The sun was not quite peeking out from the darkness when Jeremiah was warming his sweet wonderful cinnamon orange bread and icing. Famous could smell the bread and the coffee. The aromas woke her senses as she gradually opened her eyes. The three little critters were still cuddled next to her and seemed dismayed by her movement. Standing and stretching she wandered in the kitchen.

Jeremiah's smile was bright, "good morning, sleepy head."

Famous smiled "It smells so yummy in here I couldn't stay asleep." Jeremiah handed her a cup of coffee and motioned her to sit down. "My mother spoke fondly of your food preparation in her journals. It's such a delight to wake up to whatever wonderful aroma you have going on in here." Jeremiah glowed at the compliment. They ate in quiet anticipation of the day to come.

Famous brushed her teeth and washed up for the trip. She braided her hair, put on a hat, and waited for Jeremiah to say he was ready. Then the journey began as her mother's had, walking to the river and heading upstream. The terrain was a gradual slope at first then as they headed up higher and it got steeper and steeper. Soon they were climbing large boulders and were nearing cliffs. In some areas Famous was scared she would fall to her death. They shimmied against rocks on small ledges. It would have been terrifying if not for the stories Jeremiah was telling about the journey with her mother in the same areas.

At one point Famous slid down some gravel, it felt as if she would never stop sliding. She tumbled and tumbled, falling, feeling as though this were the end and as if by magic she stopped. It felt as if she were lifted to her feet by a gentle hand. She glanced around but Jeremiah was several yards above her. He looked back to her and smiled. The climb back up was nerve racking, she would climb several feet then slide back. She thought of life and the struggles one goes through, this is very much like that. Thinking how you go forward and circumstances may knock you back, but you must dredge on.

The sun was sinking low in the sky and Jeremiah looked concerned, "Famous we must get tucked in before it gets dark, come on we must hurry." He grabbed her hand and pulled her along scrambling towards what looked to be a cave in a crevice high up on a ledge. "That is where we will be safe for the night."

Famous looked up with horror at the thought of climbing the face of the rock. "I...I...I don't think I can make it up there."

"Of course you can, now come on we will make it. Trust me you would rather be up there when the sun sets." That scared Famous, she followed him closely to the base of the rock. He reached into his pocket and pulled out what looked to be a teeny tiny pick ax with a wave of his hand it was normal size. "We must go Famous, hurry." He kept looking back so Famous would look back, she could only see trees.

Jeremiah was attaching a rope to her and to himself. Famous could hear something, possibly growling, it could have been the wind, or her imagination. Jeremiah was rushing her as he dug the ax into a crack in the rock. He began to climb tugging on the line "Famous, watch me, place your hands in the crevices, there are places for your feet. Don't worry child I won't let you fall. I'm afraid I'm not strong enough to save you from what's coming, you really must start climbing." Terror struck her as the words resonated in her ears, she began to scurry up the face of the rock following just below Jeremiah. She couldn't think, she was so scared that she wouldn't have known what to think anyway.

Famous kept glancing behind her, she couldn't see anything. It was getting darker and darker. She looked back again and lost her grip. A scream escaped her lips and as if he had known it was going to happen he pulled the rope tight and spoke calming words. "You will be fine Famous, I have you, just regain yourself and get back to the rock." It was sheer terror for her and she wondered if this is what her mother had done. If she had read about this in her journal she certainly wouldn't have wanted to make this journey.

At long last after an hour of climbing in the dark they made it to the cave. Famous could hear echoes of growling, but it could be her all in her mind because of the trauma she had just gone through. Jeremiah busied himself with building a fire setting up things for dinner. He was singing like it had been a merry day. Famous was not feeling like singing. She was in horror and now the realization that tomorrow she would either have to climb up or go back down was settling in. A realization she was about to voice her concerns to Jeremiah.

"Famous come sit and have some dinner." His tone was pleasant and calm. She felt like, if words had came from her lips she would be screeching. She stumbled over to sit near the fire. He had laid out a blanket and it looked like a lovely picnic as if nothing had happened. It was as if there wasn't something following or actually chasing them. She had taken a few bites of the tastiest smoked salmon she had ever had. Finally she was beginning to calm. Her nerves, which she thought had been rattled beyond repair, were finally normalizing. Her heartbeat was stabilizing. "Are you feeling okay Famous? You look like you're getting your color back."

"What was that? How are we going to get out of here? What...?" Her voice trailed off to something inaudible. Jeremiah added some more food to her plate that she mindlessly nibbled on.

As the evening wore on Jeremiah prattled on about the day they had had and how it was the toughest part of the journey. "Glad to get it over with," he said. But Famous knew they were only half way up. She was all too aware that tomorrow would be just as much a challenge.

It seemed like she had no sooner laid her head on her pack when she was awakened by the smell of bacon and coffee. It was still very dark she thought as she opened her eyes. She could hear that Jeremiah was chatting, at first she thought to himself, until she heard another voice. It was a female voice, very soft, a tiny little voice, Famous strained to hear it. Jeremiah said something about a rockslide or it sounded like that. Then the female voice, it was so small and muted by the bacon sizzling. Famous sat up quickly looking over at Jeremiah.

"I could have sworn I heard you talking to someone." Jeremiah said nothing while handing her coffee and a plate. The plate had a croissant filled with bacon, tomato, cheese, and an egg. It was scrumptious. Between bites Famous said, "I heard a female voice, I know I heard it." He raised his eyebrows as if giving her a questioning look. "Perhaps I was still dreaming." She shook her head but stared at Jeremiah as if waiting for him to say something.

"How's your coffee?"

"It's delicious, do I taste vanilla?"

"Yes and just a dash of nutmeg and how about that croissant?" His voice was cheery, and he seemed quite pleased with the morning.

"Simply perfect as all of your meals. I find myself wondering what you will serve next. Even in a damp and dark cave you're able to prepare amazing dishes." She could tell it gave him great joy to cook, but even greater if it was for someone else.

"Well we have another long day ahead of us, I guess I had better get things cleaned up and ready to go."

Famous looked around the cave, she had thought was more like a big hole in the side of a rock. However, now that there was a little light she could see it was a cave. To where, she wasn't sure, and was thinking she was not too eager to go into the depths of that darkness to find out. Little did she know, that was exactly where she was going to go.

CHAPTER TEN

SIMPLY MAJESTIC

Famous tried to help Jeremiah, but he would have none of it. He shooed her away telling her to look outside and see how high she had climbed. That didn't sound at all appealing to her. "You may as well look Famous we won't be leaving that way so it will be your only chance." She instantly knew what he was saying looking behind him into what she had been thinking was probably the depths of hell. An extreme exaggeration on her part.

Famous walked to the edge of the cave and looked out. Running back to get her camera, "It's simply majestic, Jeremiah, I don't think I've ever seen anything so beautiful in all of my life!" She exclaimed.

Walking back toward the edge she wasn't watching where she was walking and tripped over a rock, almost sending her over the edge. Jeremiah had grabbed her just in time. Famous didn't know how he had gotten to her from where he had been standing, but she was truly grateful he had. "You must pay attention silly girl, now take your pictures, it's time to go."

Famous marveled at the valley below and though shaken from her near death experience it did not distract from the breathless awe of the view. She was certain she could see for miles and although she knew she couldn't truly capture the feeling or even the beauty of it, she took a dozen pictures. These were the times she missed her mother the most. They had shared these feelings of awe on many trips. Inside, Famous knew she had been here and they were still sharing just at different times. Her mother had brought her here to share even if she couldn't be here to share it at the same time.

Jeremiah could see that Famous had gotten what Dar had wanted her to experience from here. So it was time to move on. He had loved Dar very much, so when she wrote him asking him to take Famous on this journey he was delighted. He couldn't wait to share with Famous the same experience and then there were the letters. He had waited for Famous to come for seven long years, he had not given up hope, but had become weary. To watch her standing on this cliff as her mother had so many years ago his eyes filled with tears of joy.

"Time to go," Famous turned wiping away her own tears and followed Jeremiah into the cave. Glancing around she could see he had everything taken care of. By now she had grown accustomed to the fact that he had a magical way of doing things. He motioned her to follow him into the darkness with just a small lantern to light their way. He calmed her by asking questions about the books she had read.

The cave was dark, she was worried about bats and rodents. He assured her that things were fine. He told her that her mother had made this journey and she came through it fine. There was beginning to be water in the cave at first a trickle, but it soon rose to her calf. The deeper it got the more nervous she became. The cave began to slope upwards and the water was rushing downhill. The floor was becoming very slick not unmanageable, but quite challenging. Making forward progress and sliding back a step or two.

Famous tumbled to her knees getting completely soaked, all she could do was laugh which made Jeremiah laugh. He slipped and like a dark water slide they slid back to the bottom with a splash. The lantern was out and they sat laughing in a puddle at the bottom in total darkness. "I'm afraid my lantern got wet."

"You think?" Famous was laughing uncontrollably. Jeremiah stood up and asked for her hand. It took several tries before they found the other's hand. He gave her a tug and helped her to her feet. Holding the lantern he gave it a shake and blew on it. The flame came to life.

"It must not have been as wet as I thought." He smiled and winked, Famous just gave him a look, like if he really wanted her to believe that he was crazy. "Shall we try again?"

Famous shrugged, "Might as well." They began again to climb the steep slick surface. Famous wasn't nervous any longer. She was having a fun adventure in a wet dark cave. "I hope I didn't get my mother's journals wet. I have them in Ziploc bags in case of rain so they should be ok."

"They are fine then, I am sure. Once we make it to the top we won't have far to get out of the cave. We can lay somethings out to dry by the campfire."

"Will we get to the waterfall today?"

Shaking his head, "No, I'm afraid not."

"That's okay, I'm rather intrigued by the journey."

Jeremiah smiled to himself as he knew that his part of her journey was only the beginning. He was happy it was going so well. Dar said it was what would give her the strength and the desire for the rest of the journey, as it had her. It was the most important part, the foundation, she had said to Jeremiah, in her letters. She knew if anyone could open her up to the world it would be him.

They slipped and slid but managed to get to the top. Famous could see a glimpse of light, it was dim but she knew it was there. It had taken most of the day and Jeremiah had said they would camp just inside the cave on the other side to be safe. There was no reason to wander in the forest so late in the day.

When they came to the end it was covered by bushes. "These have certainly grown over since I was here last." He chuckled as he cleared some bushes so they could walk out. It opened to a cove where there were several deer drinking from a small creek. They glanced at Famous and Jeremiah and began drinking again. She laid her pack on the ground retrieving her camera, suddenly grateful she had opted for the water-proof one. She had told herself just in case she ever wanted to take pictures underwater she wanted the option. There were bunnies, deer, and even moose. Taking pictures of everything like it was the first time she had seen these creatures.

Famous set up her tripod, set the timer and took some pictures. Pictures of her and Jeremiah, first with the animals in the background and then the cave. Their clothes were still soaked so Famous changed and laid her things out to dry, grateful her Ziplocs had held strong.

Jeremiah cleared more brush from the cave to ventilate the smoke and started a fire. They were super hungry from the days' travels and missing lunch. Jeremiah was fast to prepare a delicious meal. He had made some dip with crabmeat and cream cheese with crackers to hold them over while he warmed some stew and bread. Famous wasn't even surprised that nothing of his was wet. The stew had large chunks of carrots, potatoes, and meat. It was just as her mother had made for her. She wondered if that's where she had gotten the recipe.

They sat near the fire talking about their day. Famous could hardly wait to write about the two days in her journal. She was quite happy they had stopped early unlike the night before. The day had been much easier like Jeremiah had said. Maybe that was truly the hardest part of their journey. Then Famous thought what happens after the waterfall? She hadn't really considered that before now. She knew it wasn't the end of the journey, but where did she go after that? There was no real point to dwell on this thought, patience Famous, you'll know as time allows. She chuckled to herself as she thought the words she had been told all of her life.

After Jeremiah turned in for the night Famous took out her journal and detailed the past two days. She had hoped if anyone read it they would feel the fear, joy, and laughter in her words. She was yawning and feeling very sleepy. When she laid down she heard a rustling noise in the bushes. She burrowed herself down in her sleeping bag. Although she was scared she couldn't keep her eyes open any longer. Her dreams were so strange she woke in a panic, but couldn't remember why. It was quiet and peaceful, she laid her head down again thinking of what the next day would be like.

CHAPTER ELEVEN

WHAT AM I DOING HERE?

"Coffee?"

Famous could hear the voice and even the word, but she didn't want to open her eyes. She was achy today. The climb, the fall, sleeping on a rock, were just a few of the reasons, and with that she was sure there were others as well. She only knew she didn't want to move. "Coffee" That's odd she didn't smell coffee. It wasn't Jeremiah's voice either. She strained to listen for the voice again. "Coffee" it was her mother waking her, she was sure it was her voice. Famous heard whispers from behind her in the cave. She sat up abruptly and looked around. Jeremiah was just now putting on the coffee.

"It sounded as if you were talking to someone."

"You're awake early," That's what he did, avoided her questions. "We have chocolate croissants for breakfast." It was always done in such a way she almost didn't realize it. Almost being the key word.

"Were you talking to someone?"

"Do you see anyone here Famous?" He did it again he didn't answer the question. She wasn't quite awake and decided to drop it for now knowing it was a losing battle. "Come have some coffee." His voice was sweet and gentle as if consoling her. She sat quietly drinking her coffee and eating her croissant as Jeremiah got his things together.

"Will we make it to the waterfall today?"

"Yes, I believe we will." His voice was cheery and he had a huge smile. "Does that please you Famous?"

"I think so, but I am a little nervous about what happens after the waterfall."

He patted her back "you'll be just fine." She smiled brightly, if she couldn't trust a wizard then who could she trust? "A few more details and we can head off on the day's adventures." Jeremiah washed and placed the last of the dishes in his pack. Famous turned her back for just a second to grab her pack and when she turned back he was heading out of the cave. "I'll be outside." He was whistling a happy tune on his way out.

The first few hours were beautiful meadows with green grass and so many flowers Famous stopped to take pictures every half hour or so. The sky was the brightest blue with not even one cloud in the sky. They saw many animals on the journey, happily playing, eating and drinking. She was amazed that the animals didn't seem to be scared of them at all. They acted as if Famous and Jeremiah belonged in the forest. They met back up with the river and began to follow it upstream. Stopping to make a snack under a nice shade tree. Famous washed her face in the water. She laid back on the grass and rested her eyes. She could hear all of the sounds of the forest. Birds, a gentle breeze, the water cascading over rocks. It was a peaceful joyous experience.

Famous got up to help Jeremiah and watched as he was petting a bunny. The bunny nuzzled him as he fed it carrots. It was a perfect picture so she snapped several. She slowly joined him and laid out the blanket. He had watermelon, oranges, apples, smoked salmon, cheese, and crackers. Such a great lunch for a picnic. They snacked and chatted for nearly an hour when he said that they had better be moving on.

An hour or so later Jeremiah pointed to a really steep hill covered with boulders. "We will climb there and just on the other side we will be on top of the waterfall so it won't be long now. A couple more hours I suppose." At the base of the hill it looked like it was going to be quite a task to climb to the top.

"Is there any other way?"

"Not that we could make today, Famous we will be fine." She tightened the straps on her pack and began to follow the wizard to the first boulder. It was a tremendous struggle as there was nothing to step on or grab hold of. Famous walked around it from side to side. She glanced left of it then right looking for some way possible. "I know there was a place to begin years ago, so there must be one now." The old wizard followed the steps Famous had just taken. "Hmm, let's see, perhaps we can walk a little further." Famous agreed.

They passed several boulders exactly the same that had no possibility of climbing. Finally they reached a crack they could shimmy up between two boulders. It was a little bit more of a struggle for Jeremiah as he wasn't as skinny as Famous, but he made it. Once on top of that boulder they had to hop back two to gain access to climb higher. It took hours of climbing in this manner to reach the top. The summit was glorious, they could see miles and miles of valleys. They could see the ocean far off in the distance. There was so many trees and grass it was absolutely stunning. Famous felt like she was on top of the world until she realized they would have to climb down by rope to get to the waterfall.

Jeremiah tied a sturdy line to a tree and secured it around his waist. Then another around hers. "I say we go down together, what do you think?" She nodded with reluctance, but followed him to the edge. "Ok, starting is the hardest part. Once we get to the waterfall we will swing into the cave that's behind it, got it?"

"Got it," she looked extremely nervous.

"If you're worried, I can lower you down instead."

"No, don't be silly, besides it might be a great photo op." He laughed handing her a pair of gloves and slipping on a pair as well he showed her how she would let out a little at a time.

"It will take some upper body strength, I sure hope I still have it in me." He chuckled as he began to crawl over the edge. Famous laid on her stomach and inched her way over the edge. The climb wasn't so bad, but there was no way she had a free hand to take a picture of Jeremiah or anything else. She lowered herself and walked down the wall at the same time. Jeremiah did the same, they had reached the waterfall in a very short time. Water was splashing Famous in the face and she was struggling to see inside. Jeremiah had swung in and landed on his feet very quickly. She was thinking that he probably cheated when he grabbed her foot and pulled her in. She landed right on top of him and they toppled to the ground laughing hysterically.

"We made it!" Jeremiah exclaimed with joy. Standing up, Famous looked around with confusion. She couldn't for the life of her figure out what was here for her. What did her mother want her to find here? She took off her backpack and searched for the journal. Jeremiah knew what Famous was doing. "So, I bet you're wondering what you are doing here? Well, I am famished, during dinner, I will tell you everything. Come let's fix some dinner together I'm afraid it will just be a hodgepodge of leftovers but it will only take a minute." She agreed and set her pack down.

CHAPTER TWELVE

THE LETTERS BEHIND THE WATERFALL

Jeremiah began the story, "When your mother had taken ill she sent me a letter asking me to take you on the same journey I had taken her on so many years before. She said she had left you her journals to follow and so I should expect you. Over time she would send me letters and always include one for you. So the thing is she wanted you to experience what she had at the beginning of her journey to finding you Famous. She said it was this beginning that gave her the strength to carry on. I have the letters with me as I am to give them to you in the morning here behind the waterfall. Tonight you must read on in the journal to find the next part in your journey."

Famous nibbled as he told the story. "I guess I understand," was all she could say. Famous needed time to process. She had a rough three days, but she guessed that was the point. It was rough, it was fun, but most importantly with Jeremiah she was safe. It was now she was aware her time with Jeremiah was coming to an end. Nothing more was said about it as they cleaned up from dinner.

Famous opened her pack and retrieved the journal. She began reading and soon realized her journey was exactly the same. That old wizard she thought. There were really no differences at all. The night of terror climbing the face of the rock, slipping down the water in the cave, climbing the boulders, and well, everything was just the same. Only her mother didn't have letters waiting for her to take on her journey. Famous read all the way to the part where her mother was having dinner with Jeremiah here behind the waterfall and found no differences. She knew that was why she didn't want her to read on.

At the bottom of the page was a note,

"Famous look outside the waterfall, go now."

She set the book down and ran to the edge holding steady to the rope, she looked out. Looking for a sign, something, just anything that would tell her what was next. She could see a valley, down below there was a large pool of water that the waterfall fell into. She could see birds, what was it she was supposed to be seeing? There was smoke coming from a large ship on the ocean and that was all.

She turned and went back to the journal turning to the next page at the top was another note.

"You will take that ship Famous, across the ocean. I'm sure Jeremiah has timed everything correctly over the past few days to be sure the ship would be there. Stop reading now until you are on the ship."

The journal snapped closed and Famous placed it back in the bag. Thinking how in the heck would she get to the ship. It's so far away. Jeremiah could see she looked troubled. "Jeremiah, how did my mother get to the ship?"

"She didn't tell you? How curious I guess she knew you could figure it out."

"Did she go back to the cottage with you first?"

He shook his head "No just to the bottom of the waterfall and then she was off."

"She left, just like that, all alone in the forest?"

Jeremiah nodded, "I begged her to come back with me I told her it wasn't safe, maybe you should come back with me." Famous walked back to the edge, looking out and she could see the ship and the general direction of where it was, but things would look quite different at ground level.

"I have to follow her journey she believed in me, so I have to believe in myself."

Jeremiah inwardly smiled knowing she had to decide for herself. He believed in her too. It was late, she knew it was time for her to get some sleep if she were going to get some distance tomorrow. Laying in the cave listening to the waterfall, her mind raced. She had no way to download a map from the internet, possibly her GPS on her phone would work. At this point she wasn't sure of anything other than that she was going to make it to the ship one way or another.

CHAPTER THIRTEEN

GOODBYES, THE WORST PART

The night went by in a blink of an eye, Famous was eager to see the letters from her mother. Although she would have no time to read them today. Today she needed to get moving as quickly as possible. Jeremiah had made her a croissant and coffee for breakfast. "You must eat as you will need your strength. I put some snacks in this bag for you and the letters from your mother. One more thing." Famous looked up from her bag. Jeremiah was smiling, "You'll need this. I gave one to your mother before she left as well." It was a compass, Famous looked elated. She hugged Jeremiah tight. He was happy and sad at the same time. He had felt the same so many years before.

Famous was so excited by the compass, she ran to the edge and watched the pointer until it was pointed directly where the ship had been the previous day. "Jeremiah, do you know how often the ship leaves?"

He shook his head, "I imagine there's one heading out every few days of the week this time of the year."

Famous grabbed some shampoo and stuck her head under the waterfall. "I don't know when my next shower will be." She giggled "Life on the go, you don't always have a great big shower available. I feel so much better about this journey, thank you so much. This compass will save my life or at least my legs from going extra miles and being lost." It felt really refreshing to wash her hair and her face. She was very nervous, but optimistic about her trek to the ship. She was wondering how many days it would take to get through the forest to the sea.

She packed the remaining stuff in her backpack and announced she was ready. Jeremiah had minimized and pocketed his stuff. "Okay young lady we will go down on this side instead so you are pointed in the right direction. Do you know your compass heading?"

"Yes but, I will double check one more time." She sounded so excited. Jeremiah was thrilled he had done exactly as Dar had wanted. She had been the daughter he had never had which made Famous the granddaughter he had never had. He watched as she checked her compass setting again. She had her backpack on and looked so eager to get moving. He smiled, walking to the edge he looked over the side to remind himself of the route he had taken with her mother.

"So we are going to climb down over there." He pointed out rocks they would use. "It's going to be a challenge, we won't have the security of the rope. If you get in trouble you'll have to push away hard and land in the water." That was a rather nerve racking thought for Famous, she really didn't want to fall to her death or take a plunge and try to swim with her backpack on.

Jeremiah told her that it really looked much more challenging than it was and began the descent. There was a small walkway along the edge of the cave behind the waterfall that led to their beginning point. It was more of a steep path than a rock face, Famous realized that Jeremiah had been teasing her about having to push off the rock. She commented on it, he laughed.

"So why didn't we come up this way?"

"That wouldn't have taught you anything, silly girl."

"Sure it would have, it would have taught me to take the easier path."

"There isn't always an easier path so it's better to learn how to handle the harder path first."

"I know, I know, I am just giving you a hard time. That whole business of pushing off the rock and such. I was kind of freaking out on the inside." Jeremiah was laughing so hard he slipped and fell on his behind which caused Famous to fall over laughing. They enjoyed a leisure walk down the path, talking and laughing. Famous was thinking of how she was going to miss him and their talks especially the ones about her mother.

She could now see why her mother wanted her to begin her journey the same as she had. If her mother had done anything differently she may never have found Famous and it all started with this wonderful wizard, of sorts.

Although the path was quite steep at times Famous enjoyed the walk very much. There were so many beautiful things to see and the sound of the water cascading into a pool of water was like music to her ears. She could see several small creatures and would stop and take pictures along the way. Everything is so amazing in the daylight, Famous was thinking, but at night it would become terrifying, that she was sure of. She would be alone like that first night.

It took a couple of hours to reach the bottom because their leisurely pace. Jeremiah set about fixing some snacks, he wanted to send her on her way with a full belly he said. As they sat there he cautioned Famous about traveling only in the daytime. It was imperative she found a safe place to sleep at night. This somewhat scared her reminding her again how it was the first night.

"Make sure you stop before dusk and build a fire to keep you warm. It will also keep the animals away, animals don't like fire." Famous wasn't sure it was animals or whatever had been following her, that he was talking about. But she also wasn't sure she wanted to know. "I'm not worried, Famous, I know you will be just fine."

"Thanks, I must admit I'm a little worried."

"And that's what will keep you aware and safe, a little fear is good for you. Alright, well, I guess it's time for goodbyes, but I'm always here should you want to come back. Please come visit and tell me of your journey just like your mother did. Goodbyes, the worst part, I say, it sure has been nice having you around." Famous hugged Jeremiah, she felt a deep sadness, but it was time to go. With tears in their eyes they walked in separate directions. Famous looked back many times until

Jeremiah had disappeared and she could no longer see him in the distance.

CHAPTER FOURTEEN

FAMOUS FOR WHAT?

The first hour Famous checked the compass every other minute. She wondered if her mother had done the same. It was suddenly so quiet without Jeremiah. She could hear every sound in the forest again. The birds were chirping, the leaves below her feet crunched, branches swayed in the wind. Looking back she couldn't see the waterfall any longer, it gave her inspiration to walk a little faster. She wasn't going to lollygag around in the forest any longer than necessary.

The later it got in the day she began looking for a place where she could hide out for the night. Knowing darkness would be coming soon and possibly rain too. The sky had starting filling with clouds which gave her a great amount of concern. Worrying about keeping a fire going now was worse than the fear she wouldn't get it lit, her earlier worry. Famous was thinking, as she walked alone in the woods, it sure gives you plenty of time to think about these type of things.

She walked for another hour and dusk was really setting in, Famous was getting panicky. She came upon what looked like it may have been some sort of teepee at one time. Some campers or hunters must have put it up. Really it was just some tree branches, but she could make it work. Luckily she thought about bringing a few of those thermal blanket things that didn't really think she would use. But her mother had always packed them when they went camping. Famous used them and some more tree branches and she was in business, so to speak.

It was dark by the time she had finished and collected some twigs and wood for her fire. Starting it was a challenge even with a lighter trying to get a flame over and over. She heard the wolves howling in the distance and was getting so scared she quickly yanked a few blank pages out of the back of her journal. It was then she was reminded of the letters from her mother. She had been so wrapped up in survival she had completely forgotten. Crumpling the paper real tight under a pile of twigs did the trick.

Pulling out some smoked salmon, her absolute favorite, with some cheese and crackers. She plucked the first letter from the stack. There were so many and carefully bundled together with a ribbon. There was a large thud sound from directly behind her makeshift shelter that made her jump. She sat still listening for another sound, but nothing. She was sure her heart was thumping as loud as the noise that caused it. She began opening the letter to push her fear away. A crack of a branch in the distance stopped her, she got up and added more branches to stoke the fire a bit. She was certain that getting some sleep was going to be a serious challenge. Sitting back down, she began opening the first letter from her mother.

My Darling Famous,

I am so sorry to have left you alone. I watch you every day now hoping I will soon have the courage to tell you how sick I really am. I suspect you are becoming suspicious. It has been such a joy being your mother. I am setting everything up for your journey, but I wonder how long it will be before you meet Jeremiah and how far you have gone since you left him. I wanted this night in the forest to be a little less scary for you. So I am writing to you as I am watching you sleep. I am visualizing you sleeping in the woods and hope you can feel my presence.

The compass was a great surprise for me and Jeremiah had promised to give you one as well. Don't worry about the monsters in your head, you must get sleep. Just travel in the day and you will be at the ship

*in two or three days. I have faith in you. I will continue
to write to you as long as I am able. I hope to have
enough for you to read one each day of your journey even
if it's just I love you. Lie down my beautiful girl and get
some rest, otherwise tomorrow will be an even longer day.*

*There is so much I long to tell you as you find you
the way I found you.*

Love forever,

Mom

Tears were streaming down Famous' cheeks
as she stared at a small photo of her mother
sitting next to her sleeping. On the back it was
dated about six months before she had died.
She carefully placed the letter back in the
envelope with the photo. She put it in the
bottom of the stack and back in the baggie to
protect it from the elements. She was so
touched and filled with love nothing seemed
scary any longer, she laid down and fell off to
sleep.

Dawn came fast as she had slept good and
had pleasant dreams of times she had with her
mother. More than dreams, they were
memories playing back like home movies. She
awoke feeling positive and happy. Her
breakfast would certainly not compare to
breakfast with Jeremiah. A simple granola bar
and an orange would have to do, saving the
food he had given her for lunches and dinners.

Famous was tempted to read her mother's letter again, but knew she needed to get going. Carefully removing her thermal blankets, which didn't seem to fold down as small as the little plastic envelopes they originally came in. She did her best to shove them back in and got everything packed as quickly as she could to get on with her hike for the day. She was incredibly grateful for the shelter it had given her the idea to be able to put up the same type of structure throughout her journey. As long as she could find some decent branches she would not have to worry about a place to lay her head at night.

The letter from her mother was exactly what she needed to give her strength to sleep through the night. She wondered what it must have been like for her mother without that. "It must have been much like my first night," she said out loud to herself. Famous Cleaned up the last few items so as not to leave anything behind. She knew it was important to leave the forest as it was. She then headed off in the direction of her compass reading.

There were several times she would have to veer off or climb steep rocks to maintain her heading, but felt like she was on the right track. Then she thought she had passed the same spot before. At that point she climbed a tree to see if she could see the ocean. It was then that she was trapped in the tree because a momma bear and her cubs came walking through. Glad to have her camera around her neck she snapped some photos, but had to wait for more than an hour in the tree for them to move along, terrified that she would be spotted she moved slowly.

Snapping one more pic was all it took for the bear to look up. Famous froze hoping the limbs of the tree hid her well enough. The bear looked like she was starting the climb up the tree, Famous was horrified, a treed animal that's what she was. One of the cubs made a noise and was running off so the momma went after her cub. Famous blew a sigh of relief. Checking her compass heading, she waited a few minutes, and climbed down from the tree, feeling stiff and achy.

Hours passed as she marched on through the woods. Making notes in her journal along the way. Drawing pictures of odd trees, filling her water at streams, and taking a leisurely lunch of a croissant, with ham and tomato, which was one of her favorites. The bag of food Jeremiah had packed for her to take was filled with all kinds of goodies. He had put chocolate muffins, cookies, stuff for sandwiches, and several little packs of various smoked meats. There was a tiny pan barely big enough to cook an egg or warm small amounts of food.

She was really happy that Jeremiah's cottage was her first stop. Famous guessed that that was her mother's plan all along, she would have known, from her own experience that she wasn't equipped with everything she had needed either. Jeremiah had added a pocket knife type of multi-tool thing and other odds and ends. The small pack clipped right onto her backpack.

She hadn't taken the time to look through it the night before because of how late she had gotten settled. She also wanted to read her mother's letter. This long lunch break was exactly what she needed. Thinking how handy it was to have the things Jeremiah had sent with her, he truly was sent from heaven. "Time to get a move on" she said loudly to herself when she heard, "Hello" from behind her. It startled her so that she jumped. Turning around there was a little boy standing very close to her.

"Well, you sure frightened me, hello right back. Where is your mommy and daddy?"

"I don't know," he said shyly.

Famous was thinking, why in the world would a little boy, who couldn't have been more than four be out in the woods all alone? She suddenly heard a woman's voice calling out the name Anthony. She looked down at him and asked, "Are you Anthony?" He nodded and yelled out to the woman.

She came through a patch of bushes. "He just got away from me, thank you, my name is Hannah." She extended a hand.

"Hello, I'm Famous."

"Famous, famous for what?"

"No, no, that's my name, it's hard to believe, but my name is actually Famous."

"Interesting, well, Famous you're perhaps the first person I have seen in many, many months."

"Oh, I'm on my way to the coast. I must say, I was a little surprised to see your little one." Famous looked down at the little boy and smiled.

"Yes, I am normally so careful to latch the door tight when we come in from collecting the eggs. I guess I didn't do such a good job of that today. Would you like to come for a cup of tea or coffee?"

"I really shouldn't, I should get a few more miles in today. You see, I have to get to the coast."

"It would sure be nice to have the company. My husband should be back any day now. He... um, had to go get some supplies."

The way she was looking around, there was just something that seemed a little off about the woman, but it could have been Famous' imagination. "I really wish I could, but I'm expected so I need to be going." Famous was feeling nervous and started to walk away. Suddenly Hannah clutched her arm and became insistent that Famous go with her. Famous yanked her arm from her hold screaming, "Let go of me!"

"You don't understand, you are not safe here."

"And that is, just one more reason why I must go!"

The woman snatched up the little boy, "You should follow me. I will lead you to safety." Famous didn't know what to do. "Just come with me." Hannah was looking around like a scared rabbit. Something moved in the bushes they both jumped.

"I should be fine, there are still several hours of daylight." Famous protested.

"Yes, and that would normally be true, but, you know what? I'm not risking mine and my son's life, the choice is yours." Hannah started walking off, it was the direction that Famous needed to go so she decided she would follow. They walked a short distance through the bushes from where Hannah had come from, into a field. Famous followed her through the field looking at her compass more frequently now. After ten minutes they came to a large ivy covered fence. Hannah opened the gate into a lovely garden.

One side was fruits and vegetables while the other was beautiful flowers. The most beautiful flowers that Famous had ever seen. On the other end of the garden was a little log cabin. Hannah shut the gate, "I truly don't know how he got out of the gate. Anthony you scared mommy to pieces, you know you're not allowed outside of the gate without mommy or daddy!"

The little boy lowered his head, "I'm sorry mommy."

She looked at Famous, "So how about that coffee?" Famous figured, she had come this far. Maybe she could get some rest, so she shrugged as if to say why not.

CHAPTER FIFTEEN

A LITTLE NERVOUS

Famous followed Hannah into the cabin. The inside was simple, but lovely. A little couch, a few arm chairs in the little living area. A table with four chairs in the dining slash kitchen area. Possibly two or three bedrooms she thought by the number of closed doors. There were flowers in vases, here and there. A few family photos on the walls. Hannah pulled out a chair for Famous at the table. She had a kettle on the wood stove that appeared to be hot and poured water into a coffee press. "Sugar?"

"Yes please."

"You really couldn't pick a more horrible time to be alone in the woods." She placed the sugar on the table. "There is a wild creature out there. My husband has gone off to track it. It's been snatching up our chickens, I was so worried that it had gotten Anthony." Hannah poured the coffee and sat at the table. "I'm scared that it's figured out how to open my gate, I just don't know what I'll do if Jack doesn't come back soon."

"How long has he been gone?"

"A few days now," she looked genuinely scared to Famous. "I hear it out there at night. At least I think I do. I'm too terrified to sleep half the time."

Famous started getting nervous, "I need to get far away from here before the daylight is gone."

"I'm afraid it won't be far enough. You can stay if you'd like and get off to an early start in the morning. You won't get too far today and you'd still have to set up camp." Famous started to regret taking that long lunch. "I think you could make it all the way to the town on the coast tomorrow if you left early enough. It would really be nice to have the company tonight."

Famous knew she was right about not making it too much further and the thought of being in the cabin sounded much safer than whatever she would come up with. "I suppose you're right. I am a little nervous, because well, I don't really know you. And the way you grabbed me in the forest, I guess I am a little nervous is all."

"I'm sure I looked like a complete lunatic, but you have no idea what it has been like here. It's crazy because we had such an amazing life here for so many years before this. It was a dream come true when Jack inherited this place. We were so happy living here and now I am terrified every minute of every day it seems."

Famous was fidgeting with her backpack and had finally decided to take it off. "You know it all seems really strange to me. I'm only passing through so I can't imagine what that's like, but maybe the monster is in your head. Maybe it's a bear or something like that." Hannah looked like she was about to explode when the front door opened. They both were startled, Hannah and Famous jumped. Little Anthony screamed, "Daddy" and ran into his father's arms, Hannah followed. After all the hugs and kisses Jack saw Famous.

"Hi there," he looked at Famous, hon who is this?"

"Oh, I'm so sorry, I was just so elated to see you. She is Famous."

"Famous for what?"

"No, no, that's her name. Famous this is my husband, Jack."

Famous stood and shook his hand, "Hello."

"That's quite an unusual name you have, isn't it?"

Famous nodded and smiled. "So, Hannah tells me that you went hunting for the mysterious creature in the woods. Did you find anything?"

Jack shook his head, "Afraid not, I found nothing unusual at all. My thinking is it's a bear, but to be honest I just don't know." Hannah began to protest. "Now honey, I'm not saying there's nothing out there. I'm just saying I couldn't find anything to prove otherwise. I still don't recommend wandering out in the forest especially after dark, but I can't give a good reason."

Hannah looked disappointed but didn't want Jack to think it was in him, "Well, I'm sure you did your best. I still think you should stay here tonight, Famous. It will be dark too soon for you to make any headway. She's on her way to the coast. I guess I don't really know much more than that."

"Oh, I'm on a journey, it's...well, it's, kind of hard to explain. My mother had taken this journey years ago and, oh, never mind it's a long story. Getting longer by the minute. I'm on my way to the coast to take the ship, in a nutshell."

Hannah smiled and said "Well you can tell us all about it over dinner." As she walked towards the kitchen. "I'm sure you are all starved."

Jack nodded, "Yeah, starved half to death," he grabbed his belly and laughed.

Hannah looked back and laughed too, "Oh, you are so silly. It sure is good to have you home. I'll sleep better tonight, for sure."

Famous enjoyed their playful interaction. She could hear Hannah busy in the kitchen. "I'm not starved, but I could eat. Can I give you a hand with anything?"

"Don't be silly, you're a guest. I am just so grateful you and Jack are here. It's been so lonely and so scary since Jack left. I'm so grateful that he has come home safe. I am still worried about what is out there in the darkness. But for tonight I'm going to forget about all of that and just enjoy the evening."

"Well that certainly sounds like a plan to me. I'm really glad that I'm home I sure did miss you and this little guy." Jack patted Anthony on the head. "Oh and Famous, I agree with Hannah that you should stay here tonight. If you wanted to wait a couple of days I could take you to the town on our horse. I have to be getting some supplies anyway."

"Well that kind of defeats the purpose, I'm on a journey and going to town is part of that journey. I'm really grateful for the offer and for letting me stay here tonight. I really do appreciate it, but I'll be traveling on at first light."

Hannah had set the table and told everyone to come to dinner. Famous was thinking how fortunate she had been so far when it came to eating, but she wasn't sure she would have the same luck here as she had had with Jeremiah. She was pleasantly surprised that Hannah was able to come up with such a great dinner for four instead of only two at the last minute. She had prepared a hamburger rice dish and a salad.

They sat at the table and chatted about Famous and her mother. She told them she was following her mother's journey and was eager to find out how and where her mother had found her. Hannah and jack had so many questions about her mother and where they lived and how she was brought up. It was the first time they had had company in a long time. And the first time Hannah had not been scared in several months.

Hannah told Famous how they had inherited the house and it came at such a good time because the income in town where they had lived was mostly generated by tourists so most jobs were only part of the time throughout the year. It was becoming more and more difficult for them to be able to pay for their rent. Now they live off the land and

Jack goes into town during season and earns enough money for the rest of the year's supplies. She was saying that she went with him, visited with family and would sometimes do some work to earn a little extra income as well. But they did spend ten months straight a year in their little cottage in the woods. "Sometimes it can be very lonely, we enjoy playing games and watching movies but sometimes I really do miss being in a town and my family."

"Yeah I have been without my Internet only a few days and I am already going crazy, I can't imagine ten months with no phone, no internet, and no TV. I'm thinking that on this journey I will probably not have the opportunity to have the Internet and phone at all times. I can't believe how dependent I am on a ridiculous smart phone."

After dinner, Famous helped clear the table and helped Hannah with the dishes. Hannah made some tea while Jack started a fire. Hannah put Anthony to bed, Famous began asking Jack about where he had gone and looked for the mysterious creature.

"Well I wandered on my horse pretty much everywhere in every direction between five and ten miles out. At night when I was camping I could hear noises that were not the same as I heard before but then again your mind can play tricks on you when you're alone in the woods. Sometimes in the darkness it's very scary but I couldn't find any tracks that were unusual. I do know that something is stealing our chickens and there have been a lot of strange noises over the last few months compared to the last several years. Could be a new pack of wolves or bears. It's hard to tell."

Famous had thought about the things he had said, "I guess it's a good thing for me that I'm leaving the forest tomorrow. But I hope for your sake that you figure it out." Hannah came back into the room and joined the conversation. "As I said earlier my first night in the forest on my way to my mom's friend's cottage," Famous had not told them that he was a wizard, "I had one night in a forest that was very scary. I felt like someone or something was following me almost chasing me. Then when I was with Jeremiah, he seemed a little skittish about traveling at night as well. He lives in the forest a day's travel from here."

The rest of the night they chatted amongst themselves, drank tea, and told stories. Famous enjoyed their company very much and thanked them for such a lovely evening. Hannah had fixed up the couch for Famous, before her and Jack turned in for the night.

Famous pulled the second letter from her mother's letters out of her pack. She carefully opened the envelope imagining her mother carefully putting the letter in the envelope.

My darling Famous,

I hope your journey has been safe so far. It is late in the evening, as I write this I am waiting for you to come home from the library. It was one of those rare occasions that you had to work late at night setting up some kind of book sale. I'm so sorry, so very sorry that I still haven't had the strength to tell you. I don't want to watch you be sad. I know it's so very selfish of me and I wish that you would never have to face this burden at all, but especially you being so young. Oh Famous, my dear sweet Famous, I'm so excited for you I only wish I could be there to take you on this journey myself. I feel like I am going to miss so much in your future. I won't be there physically, but know I am there. In many ways you having my journal and following my adventure I get some peace, just know, that I am there with you. There are many friends you will meet and make all along the way. You will learn more about me and find yourself as I found you so many years ago.

I have enclosed a small picture of myself today and will try to do this every day until I can no longer bear to see myself in a picture.

I love you so very much,
Mom

Famous stared at the photo for several minutes. Tears streamed down her face. Thinking that this was such an amazing gift that her mother had left for her. She folded the letter and put it with the picture back in the envelope. Feeling her mother's presence as she closed her eyes to sleep.

CHAPTER SIXTEEN

DON'T PANIC

Famous was up before day break. She left a note for Hannah and Jack, thanking them for their hospitality. She apologized for not being there when they woke up but she wanted to get the most distance she could from her day. Right as the sun barely peaked through the trees she was on her way. Carefully checking her compass for the correct direction. It was still somewhat dark or dusky so Famous was nervous at every noise. Her imagination started running wild. She was afraid and certain again that she was being followed. The sound of something in the distance. She stopped to listen, but the noises seemed to stop when she did.

Walking fast again she could hear it, she stopped, and nothing. Again and again, her nerves were at the end, there was definitely something following her. Famous started to run, nearly panic stricken. Deep inside she knew that panicking was the worst thing she could do. It wasn't long before she tripped over a tree root. She slammed down hard on the ground.

Famous laid there for several minutes, finally sitting up to assess the damage. She was bruised but not broken. A noise in some nearby bushes startled her to her feet. Famous started walking at a brisk pace, looking back, she saw a fawn and its mother. She had to laugh at herself and the monsters in her head. She walked for hours trying to put distance between herself and whatever lurked in the depths of the forest.

Walking for hours, which felt like days, Famous came to a ravine with a river too deep to cross. The water was rushing very fast and she didn't know which way to go. According to her compass she had to head straight across the river. It seemed like a good time to sit down and have some lunch and think about her dilemma. Without a map she didn't know if she should go upstream or downstream. She studied the compass while eating some crackers and cheese. There was no doubt about it the most direct route was straight across. From somewhere in the distance she heard a voice, it was a soft voice and she tried to listen to what it was saying. She couldn't tell where the voice was coming from. She was thinking that it may be in her head.

Famous looked all around but could not see anyone. She thought she must have been hearing things. Once again a soft voice in the distance sounded like it was calling her name. But there was no one there. She was certain the voice was coming from upstream. Famous quickly finished her lunch and began walking upstream paying careful attention to her compass hoping not to get too far off track. If the river were to curve back in the direction of which she came she would certainly have to turn back.

An hour had passed, she could not find a way across the river. Famous knew that every step she took, she was going to have to go back on the other side of the river. It was looking like she was not going to make it to town today but she was hopeful that she could at least get across the river. Hoping the river would separate her from whatever is lingering deep in the forest and thinking there were only about five hours left of daylight. She figured she could travel for another three or so hours before concentrating on where she would be sleeping. Her mind was racing, she began to walk faster. Looking for any alternative to get across that river. She had thought about trying to swim it, but did not want to get her backpack wet.

Another hour had passed, now she was getting very concerned and nearly in tears. A voice whispered to her, this is part of the journey, sometimes it is hard to reach a goal but you can never give up. She knew this was just the voice of her mother inside her head calling to her, loving her, and reassuring her. Famous knew that her mother couldn't possibly be there, but felt like they were occupying the same space at different times, but still being a world apart.

Famous pushed ahead, somehow she knew she was going in the right direction as she came to a bend in the river and the water shallowed. Although the water was rushing she felt this was her only chance. Hoping not to get too wet she rolled her pants legs up and began to cross. The water was nearly above her knee and she was struggling with the current. At one point she thought about turning back, the rocks were so slick it was everything she could do to not slip all the way into the water.

She was nearly two thirds of the way when she stepped on a fish. The fish squirmed and swam off sending her into the water. Famous stood back up and scrambled to land. Now she was soaking wet and hoping her backpack didn't get too much water in it. She immediately dumped the contents on a dry patch of ground making sure the journals were still dry. It was now she realized she had no dry clothes and would be freezing at nightfall if she didn't set up camp and get a fire going immediately. She hung her clothes on nearby trees.

Not far from the river was a tree that had grown in the oddest of ways. She remembered reading a story about the Indians marking safe paths by tying young trees down causing them to grow curved and wondered if this was such a case. At any rate, it looked perfect for Famous to build a fort for the night.

She was busy collecting branches and twigs for her fire when she heard a horse in the distance galloping hard and it sounded like it was coming right in her direction. She wasn't sure if she should try to hide, but all of her stuff was hanging from branches and lying about on the ground. There was nothing she could do but be prepared for the worst and hope for the best.

The sound was getting closer and closer, there was nowhere to hide. She didn't think she would have time to collect all of her things, all she could only hope that they would pass by her or be friendly. Famous readied herself with her knife in her pocket hoping not to have to use it. She snatched up her and her mother's journals and placed them near the tree where she was making her fort. As she scrambled to grab her clothes off the branches her heart was racing. The horse came to a halt as she heard the man say, "Whoa."

"Well, hello there miss."

Famous tried to smile as she looked up to see the man on the horse, "Hello." He looked to be in his fifties, maybe a little older from what she could tell.

"What's a pretty little girl like you doing out here in the forest all alone?"

Famous was reluctant to say anything. "I... I am on my way to the coast."

He climbed off his horse and smiled, "You shouldn't be out here all alone."

"I'll be okay, thank you." She tried to sound fearless.

"I was just on my way back to my farm it's still quite a ways, I was thinking about camping out for the night myself."

"Well, I will probably move a little further today." Famous fidgeted as she was picking up her things.

"It sure looks like you were setting up camp for the night."

Famous started to get nervous, "I had to dry some of my clothes and now I'm just packing up."

"They still look soaked to me," He could see she was nervous. "Look I don't mean you any harm, ma'am, I just thought you could use the company, it gets mighty scary alone in these woods at night. Oh, where's my manners, I'm Joe."

"My name is Famous."

"Are you Dar's girl?"

Famous looked shocked, "You knew my mom?"

"Well, I met her a time or two anyway."

"When?"

"Years ago at Jeremiah's cottage, before you were born, I imagine."

Famous started thinking that this wasn't coincidence and Jeremiah had sent him off looking to check on her. "How did you make the connection, I don't exactly look like her?"

"I see that old rascal Jeremiah every couple of days, he told me you were coming soon. He's talked about your mama for years. I gotta be honest I'd never heard of anyone else being named Famous in my life so..." he trailed off as if there was no need to finish his sentence.

She was staring at him in silence for a minute trying to think of what to say. She knew her name wasn't normal she couldn't dispute that. "So what brings you through here?"

"I had some business in town, how about I get a fire started and we can talk all about it?"

Famous was curious about this man, she remembered a farmer in the journal the night of 'the incident' so she thought maybe she should let him stay. Then she thought about it, it was not like she could make him leave. "I guess that would be alright."

"I have some food in my backpack it's more than enough for two. I see you found a good spot to set up camp." Famous didn't answer, she just watched as he walked over and dug out a place for the fire. Noting that she should dig a hole before starting a fire. She wanted to look busy so decided to hang her clothes on a tree near the fire. She noticed it took him a lot less time to build a good fire than it did her. He pulled several items out of his backpack. He had some home baked bread and stew.

She pulled some snacks out of her bag and laid everything out like a picnic while he warmed the stew on the fire. As she took one bite, she knew for sure that that bite had confirmed her suspicions, "Jeremiah sent you out here to check on me, didn't he?"

"No, what makes you say that?" She could tell he was lying because he wasn't very good at it. "I told you I had business in town and I'm on my way back."

"This is Jeremiah's stew, I'd know it anywhere!" She was smiling, "He was worried and sent you to check on me."

"Now Famous, I don't know where you are coming up with this. Are you saying I can't make this good of stew? Maybe, I used his recipe."

"And you took it all the way to the coast and back? Come on, really? You may as well fess up."

"I told him you were too smart just like your mama was."

"Did you check on my mom?"

"Yes and no, I followed her all the way, just like I've been following you. I got to say I got a little nervous about that lady. I was about to rush in when she grabbed your arm."

"I can't believe I didn't hear your horse."

"Well, I kept my distance and walked slow. I didn't want you to catch me the way your mama did. I thought I was home free, but something spooked my horse today and sent him charging in your direction. Now I do have to tell you that I didn't and expect you to be out so early this morning. It was me you heard earlier, I nearly jumped off my horse when you tripped over that tree root."

"You said, my mom caught you?"

"Yep, she sure did, it was a little further upstream. I rode up a ways and planned to cross ahead of her. I don't know how she saw me, but she did and she recognized me because we had met. I tried to give her a story, but I guess I'm not a good liar. Today I went quite a bit further up so you wouldn't see me and if my horse hadn't spooked I might have got away with it. But, it turned out to be a nice night, we talked about her journey to find a little baby girl. I had to ask her how she knew there was a little girl waiting."

"And what did she say?"

"She said she saw you in her dreams and heard you calling for her. Your mama was quite special, I knew that right off. Jeremiah has shared your whole life with me. I feel like I know everything about you. All of these years through Dar's letters and pictures. It's nice to finally meet you."

"Nice to meet you too… wait… you said your horse got spooked. What was it that spooked your horse?"

CHAPTER SEVENTEEN

Everything is Parallel

Joe looked at Famous for a minute before answering. She guessed he was trying to think back to the moment when his horse had gotten spooked. He shrugged, "I don't really know, one minute he was fine and the next off his rocker. He definitely took off like a bolt of lightning. Who knows, could have been a bear, a wolf, I'm not sure. Horses can sense things we humans can't."

Joe took the opportunity to set up a tent-like structure over the tree. Making sleeping arrangements for both of them near separate trees. He brushed off his hands and said, "That should do us fine."

Famous interrupted him, "The woman I stayed with last night is convinced there is some kind of monster out here."

"Rumors silly girl, just rumors. There are plenty of normal dangerous creatures out here, there's no need to fill your head with that nonsense."

The sun was going down and the chill was setting in. Famous stoked the fire while Joe added more branches. She smiled, picturing her mother so many years ago sitting by a fire with Joe. Talking about her and thinking the last few days were about her and the beginning of it all.

Joe could tell Famous was deep in thought. "What's going on in that head of yours, Famous?"

"Just thinking about my mom and how everything is parallel. It probably sounds silly."

"No, not at all. It's like she is giving you the guided tour."

"I could swear I heard her voice several times in the last few days."

"I wouldn't put it past your mom to find a loophole from heaven." They both laughed.

"Yeah, it would be just like her to break all the cosmic rules of the universe."

They chatted about Jeremiah and her mom. She told him about the library. Her fears of not being able to communicate with the outside world in the last few days. Joe assured her that there were several restaurants in town she could get free Wi-Fi and get connected. The thought of tomorrow and civilization thrilled her. Joe handed her some banana bread packed with walnuts. Somehow every morsel she ate made her think of her mother. The sweet smell filled her nostrils as she took a bite. "Jeremiah's bread?"

"Now, I'm really offended Famous, how do you know I didn't bake this?"

"It has Jeremiah written all over it."

He laughed, "I can't bake myself out of a box. I'd probably starve if it weren't for him. I take ingredients to him regularly. One time, I was sure I was just taking advantage of his kindness, so I insisted in bringing extra. So he keeps half for his hard work. He says he's just happy to have the company. I don't know how he does it, everything he cooks or bakes tastes like heaven. Flavors you can't imagine together. I'd weigh a thousand pounds if I didn't have a farm to run."

Famous laughed, "I know, right. I was worried I'd gain weight with the way he fed me, but he kept me so busy. Thank goodness for that."

The moon was high in the sky, they sat in silence drinking tea and enjoying the night air. The horse seemed restless so Joe went to calm him. His behavior became erratic. He was stomping and bucking trying to get loose from where he was tied. Famous had a look of terror. Joe talked to him trying to calm him. Famous heard a branch behind her break sending her running toward Joe. His horse broke free and ran away. Famous opened her mouth to speak, but Joe pressed his finger to her lips. He took her hand and walked her over to the fire. Mouthing the words 'stay here' and handing her a branch that he had lit the end on fire.

Famous sat with her back to the fire. Staring out into the darkness. Unorganized and chaotic thoughts running through her head. She heard several shots from a shot gun in the distance. Each one caused her to jump. The thumping in her chest and the deafening sound of silence were excruciating. There are no words to describe the fear she was feeling. Probably only minutes passed, but she was sure it felt like hours before she heard something in the brush. The noise grew louder, she wanted to yell out, but no sound escaped her lips. She was frozen with fear.

It became silent again, only the sounds of the night surrounded her. The crackling of the fire, rustling of the wind in the trees, an occasional owl in the distance, it was mind numbing. Joe's horse came out of the brush giving Famous heart palpitations. He strolled near her so she stood and petted his mane. Gently talking to him gave her a calm feeling. She felt like whatever spooked him must be gone, but where was Joe? The question kept replaying in her head. Should she yell his name? Should she look for him? No definitely not, leaving the campfire would be idiotic, she thought.

Inhale, exhale, inhale, exhale, she was now having to remind herself to breath. "Joe," she had found her voice. Again louder, this time she yelled his name. After several attempts she slumped back down near the fire. She had no clue what to do. Several minutes turned into an hour when he seemed to appear from nowhere. "Where have you been? Was that you shooting?"

He looked disheveled as he sat near the fire. "I can't even describe it, I thought I had seen the biggest grizzly that ever existed. I shot, there was no way I missed. I swear he was in my sights, it looked like he went down after several shots. I slowly went to investigate and there was nothing, nothing, how is that possible? I saw it fall, at least I think I did, it makes no sense."

Joe looked to be staring in the fire, looking for answers where there were none. Famous couldn't think of anything to say. She sat there also staring in the fire, "What could it have been?"

"I just don't know, I have no explanation for what happened tonight. I'll take another look in the morning. I think I better ride you into town first thing." Famous started to protest, but felt it was a losing battle. Maybe after they got some much needed sleep. Though she couldn't imagine sleeping now. "You should get some rest." Joe's tone of voice sounded more like an order than a suggestion.

Famous looked at the tent, but didn't move. She was weighing her options. She had had a long day and it was difficult to think. "Yeah, I guess I should." She walked over and placed her sleeping bag under the cover. Debating on reading another letter from her mom, but she was so exhausted she fell asleep before making a final decision.

CHAPTER EIGHTEEN

THE SAME PATH, BUT COMPLETELY DIFFERENT

It was a restless night of sleep for Famous. Waking up every few hours and thinking about what was out there. Then thinking tomorrow will be a new day. She will be leaving the forest and that was enough for her to drift back off to sleep.

It had rained at some point in the night and Famous was grateful she had put her clothes in the tent before bed. The smell of pine trees and coffee filled her senses. A good stretch and a cup of coffee is all anyone needs in the morning. She smiled at the thought. The sun hadn't quite risen through the trees so the world was still dimly lit. Walking out she saw Joe and wondered if he had left that spot since she left him last night.

"Well, good morning, Famous, I didn't think you'd beat the sun up. Like some coffee?"

"Yes please, I have been thinking I would hurry and get packed up and be on my way. I know you want to go and see what you shot at last night so don't worry about me."

"Jeremiah would kill me, or worse."

"Worse? What could possibly be worse?"

He shook his head and handed her a cup of coffee. "I can just ride you on my horse, it won't take long."

"But, my mom, the journey, and..."

"Listen, kiddo, you have gotten all you needed from this forest. I know your mom would want you to put your safety first, we are talking about a difference of a half of a day. You are not cutting days off your journey, just hours. Remember this is also your journey. There will be times it will become about what you need from it, not what she got from it."

"That's true and I could get a few things done."

He smiled, "that's the spirit, besides everyone's journey can follow the same path and still be completely different. I have some things to pick up in town and I want to get in touch with the Rangers. So it is better for me as well."

Famous sat sipping her coffee while Joe was pulling down the tents. "Hey, don't worry about that, I will pack up, I just wanted to enjoy this fabulous coffee." He glanced back at her and went back to work. Famous started to clean the campsite. "Have you eaten?" He shook his head no, so she got out the last of the banana bread and cinnamon, orange bread. "Let's have a little food then I can be ready in less than fifteen."

"Sounds good."

Famous took a bite of the cinnamon, orange bread, "Man am I going to miss this."

"Jeremiah's cooking?" She nodded. "Yeah, probably why I've never moved." They both laughed. The sun had risen enough to give them adequate light to make sure they left the forest as clean as they had found it. Joe doused the fire with river water and covered the shallow fire pit with dirt. "That ought to do it. Ever rode a horse before?"

She shook her head, "No, but there's a first time for everything."

"Yes ma'am, I'm thinking I might ride past that area I was shooting in last night, unless..."

"I think that's a great idea." She was excited to see if there was anything there. It had crossed her mind to ask, but was going to wait until they were about to mount up. "I'm so curious."

"I'd like to pick up my casings too."

"How many shots? I mean I heard them, but I was so scared, every time you shot, it startled me, but I didn't think to count. Funny how everything seems so much scarier at night." He was so busy getting stuff together and she was still prattling along that he never answered her question.

"You ready?"

She was shoving the last few items into her backpack and clipping on the pack Jeremiah had given her. "Yes sir," Famous had felt a surge of energy and happiness all morning. She wasn't sure the reason, but she felt great. She was excited for the day, a little nervous about the horse, but she knew she was safe with Joe. He jumped on the horse and motioned for her to hand him his pack. He settled it in front of him.

"Okay, I'm going to pull you up, are you ready?" Her smile was beaming. "We're going to work together, you have to kind of jump." She took his hand and he pulled, she jumped and she fell backwards on her backpack. "Maybe you should hand that up first, I'll give it to you to put back on you once we get you up here."

"Hey maybe I should stand on that bent tree."

He nodded, "Great idea."

Famous climbed up and held a branch to steady herself. Joe got so close and it was as easy as that, she slid right on. "That wasn't so bad."

Joe pulled the reigns and they started galloping in the direction he had been shooting last night. Famous was looking at everything, it was exciting being on a horse for the first time. Joe noticed one of his shell casings and he slowed the horse to a walk. He pointed at them but continued to search the perimeter. "I know I couldn't have missed. I mean it was dark, but…" He saw something red, Famous, does that look like blood?"

"It might be, maybe we should check it out." He agreed, Joe jumped down from the horse and held out his arms to catch her. "The only bad thing is getting me back up there." She said with a chuckle.

"Awe, don't you worry we will work it out." She guessed his horse must be trained because he rarely seemed to tie up to anything. Joe ran his hand over the red liquid, "Sure looks like blood."

"Let's follow it."

"You wait here and I will go get my casings and then we can follow it."

She was looking at him, "Or we can both go get your casings and then follow the blood trail."

He chuckled and motioned her to follow him. They walked back about ten minutes to get back to them. They found all six and began the walk back in the opposite direction towards the trail of blood. It was a nice day, the sun was shining, there was a nice breeze, not too hot, not too cold, and just a typical summer/fall day. Famous was thoroughly enjoying the day. They came to the blood droplets and began to follow them until they disappeared.

"That's weird."

"Uh huh." They looked in every direction and nothing. "Maybe whatever it was had been carried off." He shrugged and took out a piece of red nylon ribbon, trackers used to mark a location so they could find it again easily, and tied it to the tree closest to the last drop. "Let's head to town, I'll tell the Rangers what happened and the coordinates. I think It's best to just leave it in their hands."

Famous pointed out a huge rock and climbed on and waited for Joe. It was a little more work this time as it wasn't as tall as the tree. After Famous was on and situated she asked "So Joe, what's your horse's name?"

"Carrot."

"Carrot, what kind of a name is that?"

"Coming from a girl named, Famous." He chuckled, "Well shortly after I got her I was preparing some vegetables to take into the farmers market and I don't know how many carrots I had in the cart but it was a lot. Every time I would get another wheel barrel full he must have been sneaking some. I had several crates of vegetables and fruit, some milk, and what not. I didn't have help that day so I didn't pay a bit of attention. Anyway when I unloaded at the market the crate had about three carrots left in it. He's lucky I have a sense of humor. I thought about naming him thief, but carrot just seemed to fit."

They rode at a steady pace chatting about farming, gardening, and cooking with fresh veggies. The conversation was pretty much only about food the last half hour of the ride. Famous was certain that hunger had set in.

CHAPTER NINETEEN

CIVILIZATION

Famous was thrilled to be back in civilization. It wasn't a super big town, but she knew she would be able to get Wi-Fi. She and Joe stopped for lunch before saying goodbye. Promising to write and a big hug. It wasn't a teary-eyed goodbye, like with Jeremiah, but she was genuinely grateful she had met him.

Famous loved the ocean, she walked along the seawall until she came to the port office. The next ship was three days out. She booked her ticket and headed off to find a nearby hotel. It didn't seem like a long walk, but she was enjoying window shopping. She was thinking about doing shopping for real once she got settled and cleaned up.

She found a hotel with Wi-Fi, laundry, and a pool. Famous paid for two nights and was delighted for the break. After checking in she went straight to her room. She noticed a bathrobe in the bathroom, it looked fluffy and soft. She took a long luxurious shower. Shaving the trees off her legs and scrubbing the forest from her body.

After her shower she wore the bathrobe to the laundry area and dumped the contents of her backpack on the floor. Tossing the backpack and all of her clothes in. She was thinking how great it was that there was no one else around because she wanted to wash all of her clothes. Even if there was anyone she wouldn't have let it stop her. The laundry room was just down the hall from her room. She had requested to be close to it for just that reason.

Once she was back in the room she noted the time and plugged in her phone. Laying back on the bed she flipped on the TV and turned on her phone. She had dozens of calls and emails from the library, her renter, neighbors, and the list went on. She got down to business answering all their questions. She had expected this and was even thinking she should call the library before she got on the ship. It was definitely not in her character to just run off.

Time went so quickly she was lucky she remembered to go put her clothes in the dryer. When she walked back in her room there was a news story on the TV about some missing people that had gone camping in the forest. She flipped to another channel, she wasn't in the mood for news.

Then she thought of her mother's letters. Pulling out the third letter, a strip of photos dropped out, it was her and her mother from one of those photo boxes at the mall. She smiled and remembered the exact day as she began to read.

Hello darling,

What a day we had today. Probably the best in a long time. Trying on clothes, eating junk food, and taking these pictures. Remember cramming in the box and making funny faces, but my favorite is the last one, the big hug. I wonder how many more hugs I will be able to give you. I'm sure it won't be enough, but I'll try to fill your hug bank before the inevitable.

Enough about me, hahaha, so how's it going? You know you can talk to me, I may not be right there, but I promise I'm always listening. As I write these letters, I read my journals and think back to where I was and try to imagine where you are. It's my third letter so you may be in the forest or in town. I don't want to ruin anything for you so I won't talk about that for now. I am feeling especially great today so I'm going to close and see if you're up for a night out.

Big hugs and love beyond compare,
Mom

She stared into her mother's eyes in the picture. "I love you too, mom" She thought back to that day, it was such a great day. After the mall they went home, she remembered sitting on her bed staring at her new clothes when her mother yelled up. "Famous, let's go somewhere, anywhere, we can go for a drive, a movie, dinner, or all of the above. You name it." Famous had her suspicions by this time. More of just a feeling that something wasn't right. She ran down the stairs and remembers saying, "I picked the mall so it's your turn to pick. Whatever you want to do is fine with me."

They drove to the beach and took a walk. Talking about everything under the sun. Went to dinner at a crab house, and then to a movie. It's funny, she thought, she could remember every detail about that day except what movie they had seen. Famous thought of every detail of that magical day and racked her brain but it just didn't come to her. She put the letter back in the envelope and placed the strip of pictures on the nightstand leaning against the clock just so she could see her mother's smile.

She knew she had to go get her laundry from the dryer. She took one more look at her mother before getting up and heading for the laundry room. On the walk back to her room she noticed a couple walking toward her in the hall. She smiled and felt her cheeks get a little flushed at the thought of running around in a bathrobe. When she reached her room she realized she had left the key card on the bed. She felt like a complete idiot returning to the laundry room she glanced around for a camera and felt sure there wasn't one, she grabbed some clothes from her clean laundry. It was one thing to walk down a few doors, but she wasn't going to the lobby in a bathrobe.

They had security let her in so she could show them her ID. How funny is that, she thought, surely there wasn't so many people that checked in today that they didn't recognize her. Policy is what it is and it was for her protection as much as theirs. Famous smiled and apologized to the man as she showed him her ID. She even attempted to tip him, but he wouldn't take it.

"It's all part of the job miss..."

"Famous, just call me Famous."

"I saw that on your driver's license, is that your real name?"

"Yep, my mom was a bit unusual." She smiled and saw him out.

Hunger was setting in so she grabbed her purse and the key card and ran out the door. Thinking of her mother she went to a crab shack near the beach. She had a vision of her mom sitting across from her, laughing and telling a story. At the time she would have thought it was a farfetched story, but now she wasn't so sure.

It seemed to her now that maybe all those fairy tales weren't fairy tales at all. It made her think back in time when she was a little girl and her mother told her of a wizard and a waterfall. A realization or a memory of some frightening tales that even though they had a happy ending, they were still scary none the less. She had to ask herself if that was what was to be her future and a not so distant future at that.

The thought had gripped her so hard she hadn't even noticed the server was asking for her order. "Ma'am?"

"Oh, I'm so sorry, lost in thought. I'll have the dinner special and water." Famous was thinking of the past week and everything that had happened. She wondered if Joe had ever figured out the mystery of the forest, but thought that there was little chance she would ever know. The server placed a plate of crab legs in front of her and for a minute Famous didn't think about anything. A short lived moment as her mind ran like a clock, never ending, and second by second.

She tried to remember the story her mother had told her about a princess on a ship, but couldn't recall the details. She had told that story so many years ago. All the stories she thought were made up or from books her mother had read, but they were stories her mother had lived. Of course as she told them there were differences, like she was a princess not just a young woman. It was a dragon in the forest instead of a bear. The wizard in her story was more mystical and magical. Although she had written several small children's books from her mother's stories there were several stories she couldn't remember.

She devoured her dinner, paid her bill, and walked back toward the hotel. Along the sea wall she stared into the depths beyond the ocean, looking at the waves, picturing her running with her mother, laughing, and singing silly songs.

She nearly jumped out of her skin when someone placed a hand on her shoulder. "Joe, holy cow, you nearly gave me a heart attack!"

"Sorry about that, by the time I finished up in town, I decided I stay for the night. I was enjoying the night sea air when I saw you. Did you get your ticket settled?"

"Yes, the ship leaves port the day after tomorrow. It's a good thing too, I'm going to have to get some warmer clothes tomorrow."

"Good idea, it's really cold where you are headed." He smiled, she sensed he knew her future. Surely he must know the whole story, she thought.

"So, you know where I am going? I mean I know where the ship is taking me of course, but the rest is a mystery."

"All in good time young lady and you will know as well. Where are you staying?"

She pointed at the hotel across the street, "And you?"

"The same, I was just about to head back."

"I'll walk with you. Did you talk to the Rangers?"

"Yeah, but right now they have some campers missing so they just wrote a report. I don't think it will be a high priority."

"I saw something about that on the news but clicked off of it. I guess I should have watched it, so, what's the story?"

"I'm not really sure. You know how it goes, they don't give a bunch of details to the average Joe that walks in with a farfetched story of a disappearing grizzly."

She was giggling, "Average Joe, that's really funny especially when your name is Joe. Yet, I doubt there is anything average about you." As they crossed the street she asked if he was interested in breakfast in the morning. He agreed to meet her and they said good night.

It was still somewhat early when she got back to her room. It was an opportunity to get caught up on writing in her journal while everything was fresh in her mind. She looked back to her last entry and had to rack her brain to detail the time between then and now. It seemed like so much had happened. How is it possible, all those years of nothing but the mundane day in and day out? Only the end of the day was filled with the color of her mother. That was the best way to describe her life was black and white with this amazing rainbow at the end, her mother. She added this at the end of her day's journal. Now she felt like had she lived in her mother's colorful world and it was full of so many emotions. It was exciting, terrifying, joyous, happy, sad, and just her mother.

So a ship to Ireland, she thought back to the day she found the journals. There was a napkin from some place in Ireland. She dumped out the contents that she had packed with the journals. She stared at the napkin, on one side was the name of some place she couldn't really tell what kind of place, probably a restaurant or pub, she imagined. On the other was some faded words written in her mom's handwriting that she couldn't understand and a set of numbers, "I guess this is where I'm headed."

She placed them back in the bag, but wrote the name down, thinking she would Google it later, it may not even exist anymore it has been years. She looked at each item as she placed them in the bag. She hadn't noticed the train ticket before, 'that would have been helpful information', the thought made her chuckle. Her mother left her all of these clues, it's time to pay a little closer attention to detail. Thinking she should really look at those items tomorrow, but for tonight she was going to lay around and watch some mind-numbing TV.

CHAPTER TWENTY

THE BEST HASH BROWNS

She woke up to the room phone ringing, she didn't even remember watching anything. She must have fallen off to sleep as soon as she clicked on the TV, she guessed. Grabbing the phone, it was Joe, setting up the time for breakfast. She glanced at the clock, thirty minutes, plenty of time for a quick shower. Standing there as the water ran down her back she thought of the days she had without a shower. The littlest things you really don't appreciate until they are gone. You really appreciate them when you get them back though.

She toweled off, got dressed, brushed her hair, and ran out the door. She finally felt like she had slept. Noting she had slept for nearly eleven hours. Joe was waiting in the lobby, "I hope you weren't waiting long." He smiled and said "Nah just a few minutes, are you ready? You could have dried your hair, I wouldn't have minded waiting."

"I prefer to let it air dry. So where are we headed?"

"A café down the block, they have the best hash browns in the world."

"Sounds like my kind of place." As they walked down the sidewalk she told him about the napkin and the train ticket even though she felt a little foolish about that.

He laughed and listened to her talk about the other items she had yet to look at. She sounded so excited and every once in a while scared, but mostly excited. Joe was thinking how much Dar would have loved to see Famous right now. In his heart he knew she was watching, did see her, and felt joy.

The café was small, only about eight tables, but they found a spot right away. Joe ordered for both of them telling her to trust him. The breakfast was amazing, it made her think of the hash browns her mom had made her on an occasional Sunday brunch day. Her mother would sneak off to the store while she was sleeping and when she would come down the stairs her mother would loudly announce it was Sunday brunch day. Which meant these amazing hash browns, eggs, bacon, sometimes sausage, and an English muffin. Then they would spend the whole day playing cards and watching movies.

"You brought my mom here!" It was a statement, not a question.

"What makes you say that?" He wasn't fooling her, she could read it all over his face.

"Don't even try to lie, my mom made these for me exactly the same. You didn't mention you had breakfast with her."

"How do you know she didn't come here on her own?"

"Really? Is that how you want to play this?"

"Fine, yes, I brought her to town, yes I stayed, and yes I took her to breakfast."

"Anything else? I mean the day is young, did you stay until she got on the ship?"

He was eating his breakfast, "You better eat that before it gets cold." She was staring at him, but didn't say anything else for a while. They ate in silence. "You know your mom sat in that same spot wondering about her fate, as I am sure you are. I told her that instead of trying to figure out the next moment she should live in this one. I guess the apple doesn't fall far from the tree. So I'm saying the same to you. It's great to have a goal, but don't lose sight of the time along the way."

She thought of that and what he had said, was she really like her mother? It was possibly the best compliment she could ever get.

"Thank you, I guess I lost sight of the journey for a moment."

"It's been a long and yet short journey so far, it happens. It happened to her, I'm sure more than once. You are your mother's daughter."

Joe insisted on buying her breakfast, "Well this is where we say good bye for real. I have to get back to the farm and I'm sure Jeremiah is waiting for my report." He gave her a big hug, "Please write, we will be waiting for every letter. Live each moment, smile often, and know you are thought of." Her eyes were full of tears as she hugged and thanked him. She started down the sidewalk toward the shops and when she looked back, he was gone.

The next couple of hours she spent getting winter wear. She knew it would be cold on the ship and even more so hiking through Ireland and beyond. She hadn't really known what to pack in the beginning so she had expected to have to buy some things along the way.

When she got back to the hotel she called the library, explaining and apologizing. Her boss was happy she was on this quest and said not to worry, she had found some temporary helpers from the high school and college. She had some pretty big shoes to fill so it took more than one person, but it was covered. She was just delighted that Famous was okay and wanted to hear all about it when she got back. Famous promised and said 'talk again soon.' As she hung up the phone she realized that her boss was the closest thing to a best friend she had had other than her mother.

Famous took a moment and wrote down some notes in her journal. She put on her suit and headed for the pool. She was amazed that it was empty and thought about how tourist season must have been coming to an end. After a few laps she went back to her room.

She thought maybe it's time for another letter from her mom.

My sweet Famous,

Well, what a time we had yesterday and last night. Thank you, a mother could never wish for a better ending to her story than the time I have with you. Right now you are still sleeping and I am so eager for you to get up. I know today is your last day off for several days so I can't wait to spend the day with you. Isn't it funny, at this point I'm sure many mothers and daughters have separate lives, but not us. I am eternally grateful. I guess I should talk to you about my condition, it just never seems to be the right time. I guess I want us to be normal for just a little longer. My heart hurts every time I think of leaving you. Oh heck, here come the water works.

Let's change the subject, you must be in town by now. Isn't it a lovely town? There is so much to say, but it's all in my journal so I guess there's no need for redundancy.

Well my beautiful girl here is my pic of the day, it's me sitting on the stairs waiting for you. Don't be sad my love, I'd wait an eternity for one more day with you.

I know you can feel my energy, I'm always with you.

Mom

Famous looked at the picture of her mom and laughed away the tears. Her mom was at the bottom of the stairs making a silly face. She imagined how many times she must have set the timer on the camera to get the perfect picture. She noticed every picture had been dated on the back to the date she had written the letter. Some she had written a little something on the back as well. On this one it said 'aren't you awake yet?' It was just like her mother to cheer her up after such an emotional moment.

The rest of her day consisted of packing and snacking. She flipped through the channels a few times, re-read the four letters she had read in the past few days. Re-read the last journal entry she had read at the waterfall. Double checked her gear and bagged the clothes she wasn't taking for a local thrift shop. She decided not to Google the place in Ireland and not to think beyond this moment. It was the here and now she needed to live. With that thought she grabbed the bag and headed out the door.

The thrift shop was not too far, she had been there earlier in the day and bought several winter clothes there. The woman was very sweet and surprised to see her back. "Hello again."

"Hi, I thought I might donate a few things I don't have room for in my backpack. I won't be needing them where I'm going." The woman was pleased to take them and thanked her. Famous walked to the door, she looked back, "I really enjoyed your shop, thank you." The woman smiled as Famous left.

Famous dropped by a convenience store and picked up a few snacks for the ship and a pizza to take back to her room. She had to be at the port semi early to check in so it was going to be an early night. She stopped by the lobby to request a wakeup call and went back to her room for the night.

When the phone rang she jumped out of bed, took her shower, and left as quickly as she could. She arrived at the port at least an hour early. Somewhere in her mind she was thanking the universe they had coffee there. After two cups and a nice chat with a few other passengers it was finally time to board. Her cabin was small, actually that was an understatement, but she didn't care, she was going to Ireland. The ship seemed to be a semi cargo/cruise ship. It was definitely not luxurious, but a cruise ship, none the less.

Famous joined the small group outside to wave good bye to the people on the shore. Her thoughts were about reading her mother's journal. Although, she knew she would wait until she was out to sea. Famous had never been on a ship like this. It was an odd drunk feeling, she kept losing her balance as she walked along the side. Grateful not to be sea sick as she saw many others that couldn't say the same.

When she got back to her cabin she opened the journal and laid down to read, when there was a knock on the door. It was the steward double checking papers and giving a schedule for the evening. She thought it was odd because she had done all of this earlier. She laid back down and grabbed the journal again.

She read through the pages, it was a journey similar to her last few days in the forest. There were many differences of course she didn't stay at Hannah's cabin and was chased by a bear, not stalked by an imaginary monster, but it was basically the same. When she turned the page another page had been stapled in.

Well how was it? I'm sure by now you know that sneaky, old Jeremiah sent Joe to babysit you like, he did me. I hope he had time to take you to breakfast. Maybe he even gave you words of wisdom. I hope you're not seasick.

Before you turn the next page, go mingle, I know it's not your character, but have a drink, do some dancing, take this time to live.

Love me, mom, in case you forgot

Famous looked in the mirror and was pretty sure that was not a good idea. She drank one time with her mother and it was a total fiasco, she danced and sang until she fell off the coffee table and sprained her ankle. Of course her mother had the video and Famous had the hangover to prove it. She hated to admit it, but she did have fun. It was hard to imagine one minute of her life that she didn't have fun with her. She tossed the journal on the bed and went to mingle.

The corridors were long and easy to get lost in. When the ship took a wave, Famous fell on her backside. A crew member happened around the corner and helped her up. "It seems, I haven't found my sea legs."

"It takes time, do you want to know a secret?" She looked up at him and smiled. "I have been aboard a couple years and I am not sure I have found mine either. Oh and be careful when they serve you food and drinks." He smiled as he pulled her up off the floor.

"Thanks, I was actually looking at getting some lunch or something. I guess I'm lost."

"I'll show you the way."

"I'm sure you are too busy for that."

"I'm here to serve." He took her along the corridor, she nearly fell several more times. At one point she fell back on him and knocked him down, they both laughed. "You were right about those sea legs."

"Oh, I'm a natural klutz, I'm sure that doesn't help." Finally after several corridors, an elevator and some stairs, they were at the pool area. There was a small buffet and a few activities. People were milling about having a good time.

Famous walked next to the pool towards the buffet. It was then that the ship rolled on another wave, a lady with a plate of food ran right into her sending food all over her clothes, knocking Famous into the pool. She popped up and grabbed the side, several young men were there to give her a hand and the one from the corridor had even jumped in. She looked around, feeling surrounded, she burst into laughter. "Oh my, this is embarrassing." She climbed out of the pool, "I think I'll be going back to my cabin."

A crew member placed a towel on her shoulders. "I'll take you ma'am, what's your cabin number?"

"103," she was still smiling.

The young man ushered her back to her room. "We will have your clothes cleaned and brought back to you, just bring them to the steward's desk. I'm truly sorry, what an unfortunate event."

"Oh there's no worries here, how can you possibly control the sea?"

"I must say, miss…?" He glanced at her waiting for her to fill in the blank.

"Famous, just call me Famous."

"Really, Famous?" She nodded and smiled. "Well, I must say Famous, you sure have an exceptional attitude about wearing someone's lunch and being forced to take a dip."

"Well, this brings back a time when I had done something at school that was too embarrassing to even remember. My mother had told me that how I react to situations will only make the situation better or worse. It was my choice. So I choose to laugh and move on."

"Your mom sounds like a smart lady."

"She was," Famous look at him sadly.

"Oh, I'm sorry."

Famous shrugged as they approached her room, "Hey thanks a bunch for not making me get lost and adding insult to injury."

"No problem, you know what, I'll send housekeeping down to grab those clothes for you."

"You don't need to do that."

He was already on the phone calling them. "Someone will be down in about a half an hour, should be enough time to grab a shower. Looking forward to seeing you around Famous."

"We'll see, I might be better off staying indoors. I'm really just on a quest to get to Ireland. But then again life is all about the journey, isn't it." He nodded and smiled as he walked away.

CHAPTER TWENTY ONE

WHERE'S YOUR LIFEJACKET?

Famous hadn't thought of having a nice dress for an evening out. She didn't even have shoes other than hiking boots. She had come to the conclusion she needed to find out if there was a shop on the ship where she could find something appropriate for the evening out. The brochures were on her nightstand, she browsed through them. There were so many activities and events, finally on the last page she found there were a few shops on board.

After housekeeping left with her clothes she made her way through the maze of corridors to the first shop. It was mostly souvenirs, some T-shirts, but nothing that would qualify as evening wear. She asked the girl at the computer and found the other store was such a store. She found a simple, but elegant black dress with black heels. The price was so ridiculous, she almost didn't buy them. But as her mom would say, this is not the time to be frugal, Famous.

Her make-up consisted of eye liner, mascara, and lipstick. After the price for the dress and shoes she refused to spend any more money on something she might only wear once. So it was going to have to do. Assessing herself in the mirror she decided that she didn't look half bad, she only hoped she could walk in the heels. That was something she didn't do on land that didn't move. She knew it would prove to be a challenge throughout the night.

Famous stumbled down toward the dining area and noticed a casino. She walked in and watched people on the machines. It was interesting to watch, but she wanted dinner. She hadn't eaten since this morning and she was hungry. Looking around, Famous thought maybe at another time she would have to try her luck.

When she reached the dining area, the man who had walked her to her room after the pool incident was seating people. "Are you still working?"

He laughed, "Yes, and after seeing you, I'm glad I am. You clean up real good, Miss Famous. You look stunning." She glowed, she had never been called stunning. He escorted her to a table that had five other people sitting at it. "You will love the show, it's quite good. Acrobatics, they are really talented. Well I guess skilled is a better word. Enjoy your dinner, let me know if I can get you anything." She thanked him as he walked away.

The table was full of chatter, introductions, it seemed everyone at the table was on the cruise by themselves. Famous was thinking that's probably why he put her at this table. Famous wasn't the chatty kind, she liked to read and usually kept to herself, for the most part. Tonight, she decided to really take part in the conversation. She talked about the library, her mom, and even talked about her time in the forest. Everyone seemed to hang on to her every word.

Someone had brought her a glass of champagne, but Famous wasn't a drinker so she took a sip here and there. It lasted the whole evening. The show was amazing and the dinner was delicious. She made a few attempts at dancing until she landed in the woman's lap that was sitting closest to the dance floor. After apologizing several times and overcoming the newest embarrassment she decided to just watch.

The crewman came over and told her she looked amazing out on the dance floor and she should give it another whirl. "Thank you..." She looked at his name tag, "Kai is that how you pronounce it?"

"Yes"

"Well, Kai, I think I have done enough damage for one day. I'm having a lovely time, no point in injuring myself or anyone else. Besides I'm not long from going to bed."

"The night is young, embrace it."

The ship must have hit a big wave, everyone on the dance floor toppled onto each other. Kai looked around and ran to assist people as the ship made another crash down. People were falling all over. A few of the chairs slid or crashed. Famous was sitting at a booth, Kai yelled back to her to stay put. She wasn't sure what to do, but didn't move at first. When the boat crashed down a third time the booth moved and it sounded like the ship was going to break apart.

Loud alarms were going off as Kai grabbed her arm and said she should follow him. She followed as best she could but kept tripping on her heels. The boat kept swaying and crashing into the waves. "I have to take off these shoes."

"No, there could be glass." He picked her up and carried her to a stairwell. "You should be safe here. Go to the top deck get a life preserver on just in case."

"Just in case of what?"

"Just go!" He ran back toward the dining area.

Famous thought for a moment, she had to get back to her cabin. The boat was jerking and crashing. She yanked the heels off her feet and ran down the corridor towards her cabin. She took the stairs instead of the elevator. It seemed like forever before she reached her cabin, panicked people were running in all directions. Famous grabbed her backpack and stuffed the journals and letters inside, but didn't bother with anything else. She put on her hiking boots and ran out the door. There was so much confusion and in that confusion no one realized that the crashing had stopped. There were obviously still big swells, but the worst seemed to be over. Well, not the worse of the confusion. She reached the top deck and noticed people standing around in lifejackets.

"Where have you been? I looked everywhere!" Famous looked back to see Kai standing there. "You don't even have a life jacket on."

"I had to get something."

"Do you have any idea how dangerous that was? You could have gotten trapped."

Famous felt like a child being scolded. "I… I… I'm sorry, it was very important."

"Worth your life?"

"To me, yes!"

The alarms stopped and crew members were assessing damage. The ship's nurse and doctor were checking on passengers.

"Kai, is it over?"

"You must stay here, promise!"

"Okay, but…"

"No buts, we need all passengers on top deck, while we check for safety. I have to go." He ran toward the stairs. Famous sat down on the deck up against the wall and watched as more and more people came up top. Several looked terrified and grabbed life jackets. They seemed to be hovering near the life boats. Several crew members were assisting the passengers with lifejackets. One came to Famous and told her she needed to put hers on.

Famous put on the lifejacket over her backpack, there was no way she would leave that behind. She immediately thought about the Titanic. She had read several books about the Titanic. She knew if anyone went in the water the lifejacket wouldn't save them from the cold waters below. She sat there for hours watching people and waiting. As the time passed, people started to calm and one by one had found a place to sit down. There was a crew member at the stairwell doors to assure no one went back down until it was cleared.

Throughout the whole episode, announcements were made, "For the safety of all passengers, please make their way to the top deck and remain on the top deck."

Famous guessed they were checking structural integrity. Many people started to complain, but Famous knew that that would do no good. That just escalated the misery. One woman sat next to her and started in when Famous calmly told her that they were just doing their jobs. And that she would only make the situation worse by moaning about it. The woman got up and left.

Famous stared up at the night sky thinking about her mom up there watching, probably knowing the outcome already. She wondered what she would be thinking right now given she was in the same predicament. She would probably try to make a game of it to lighten the mood. Famous smiled.

"What are you so happy about?" Famous looked up and it was the crew member that had shown her to the pool. "You were smiling, while everyone else is, well obviously not."

"I was just thinking, oh I'm Famous, you aren't wearing a name tag."

"Alex"

"Alex, you're the first one who didn't ask about my name."

"Oh I had heard your name was Famous, pretty weird name."

"Excuse me? Don't worry, I'm kidding it is a weird name. So what's up?"

He smiled and was all nonchalant, "Me, oh not much, how about you?"

"I came out to watch the stars, maybe take a stroll on the deck, I had no idea all these other people would get the same idea."

"I like you Famous, so much so, that when we get the all clear, I'll give you a five minute head start."

"Mighty kind of you Alex."

"Wouldn't want my favorite passenger to get trampled. I guess I better get to it, I just saw you sitting here smiling away. As if you had not a care in the world."

"That's how I roll," which wasn't exactly true, but she was trying. "So are you saying I should have a care or there's going to be an all clear on the horizon?"

He shrugged, "Beats me, I just work here."

Famous thought about getting up, her butt was falling asleep, but she didn't want to push through the crowd of misery. Also, she was looking forward to that five minute head start and wanted to be sure Alex could find her. She leaned back and closed her eyes for a few minutes. Alex touched her shoulder and it startled her.

"Sorry, but are you ready for your five minutes?"

"Really?"

"Yeah, go, hurry, they will be making the announcement soon. I'll walk in front of you and give you cover. As they approached the stairs the crewmember watching the stairs started to protest when Alex whispered something in his ear. "Famous after you are out of sight hand out the lifejacket." She stepped down two stairs and peeled it off. "Go, run, you only have a minute or two before the corridors will become a nightmare."

Famous ran down the stairs as quick as she could she was on the last set of stairs when she heard the announcement. She didn't see even one person before she was safely in her cabin shutting the door. She thought to herself, sometimes it pays to be nice. Famous was full of adrenaline, she took out her journal and wrote pages and pages about her day. What an eventful day she had, dining, dancing, well kind of dancing, the pool incident, and her two new friends Alex and Kai. All and all a great experience, well except for the whole boat thing. She laughed to herself. When she laid down it took only seconds to fall asleep.

CHAPTER TWENTY TWO

BINGO

It was nearly noon when she woke up starving. Famous wrapped her hair up in a clip and went out to join the world. It was real quiet in the corridor, she made her way to the pool area. A few people were out and about, but a lot less than the day before. She walked over to the buffet and filled her plate with fruit. She found a nice quiet table to drink her coffee and eat. She noticed a few areas that had been taped off, she guessed they were deemed too dangerous.

After she ate, Famous wandered around the ship deck watching the waves. It seemed somewhat ominous, not like the day before. The mood just wasn't the same. Famous looked at things differently, she wasn't going to ruin the rest of her trip being upset about yesterday. Today was a whole new day and besides other than a few minutes, well maybe more than a few, yesterday was pretty great.

"Did you get some sleep?" Kai said as she was walking past the steward's desk.

"Yes, I slept great, thanks for asking. How about you?"

"I closed my eyes for a few minutes myself. Glad to see you're out and about. Sorry for yelling at you last night."

"You were just looking out for me. Thanks for that."

"It scared me when I couldn't find you. Well I have to get back to work."

"Talk to you later?" He smiled and nodded. Famous wandered to the souvenir shop and looked around. She read a few of the T-shirts, looked at the jewelry and saw the new book titles. She thought that maybe she should get a new book. She hadn't been reading nearly as much as she was used to. Famous picked each one up and read the back before finally selecting an adventure story. There was a lot of other little nick knacks to look at. When she heard an announcement that they'd be playing bingo in fifteen minutes. She had always liked bingo, she had gone several times with her mom. She paid for her book and wandered up to the deck where the bingo was being set up.

There were a lot more people out now. Famous waited in line to get her bingo cards. She sat down at an empty table, but it didn't take to long for a few others to join her. She recognized two from her dinner table last night. They chatted back and forth until the bingo announcer started telling the rules and prizes. Some were monetary, while others were gift certificates for various shops or services, like a massage or spa day, on the ship. Each prize was written on a card and placed in a box so when you got bingo you would reach in the box to pick your prize. Famous liked the whole surprise of it.

The announcer called numbers until bingo was yelled by someone, the first game Famous didn't even get close. The second game she was one number away when someone yelled bingo. The third game and fourth games she got close, but again she heard someone yell bingo. On the fifth game, blackout, she won. She was thrilled as she went to the front of the group and put her hand in the box and pulled out a card. She handed it to the caller, "What's your name sweetie?"

"Famous."

"Well Famous, what are you hoping for?"

"Oh, gee, I don't know. Just winning was pretty cool."

"Okay, well let me take a look," The caller showed the assistant to verify the card. It was like this every time to build up anticipation. "Well, Famous you won a pretty great prize, you've won five hundred dollars."

"Really? I can't believe it, wow, that is so awesome!" She exclaimed.

"At the end of bingo please see the lovely Louise to collect your prize." Famous took her card and went back to her seat. She played the last few games, she didn't win any more, but she had a blast. At the end, she collected her five hundred in cash. She was ecstatic, thinking she won almost double what she spent on the dress and shoes.

On her way back to stash the cash in her cabin she dropped by the casino. It didn't take long to lose twenty bucks so she lost interest and went to her cabin for a little rest and relaxation. She sat at the edge of her bed and took out her mom's journal. Well she didn't exactly have a drink and dance, but she certainly did live a little. At least enough to justify reading on in the journal. A lot had happened in the last twenty-four hours.

Today, I boarded for Ireland, I sometimes wonder where this journey will take me. I had a lot of fun today on the ship. I was fortunate enough to get in with a group of singles, we sang and danced until two in the morning. I should probably get some rest now because tomorrow is another day.

It looked like she skipped a day based on the dates at the top.

Yesterday was unbelievable, it poured down rain all day. I met some ladies and they taught me how to play a card game, bridge. I ate so much food, drank too much wine and barely remembered getting back to my room. I felt so horrible this morning, and that is why I should know better. I guess we are all allowed to make mistakes and I am certainly paying for mine.

Famous turned the page and there was another note from her mom.

Hey there sweet girl,

I so wanted this part of your journey to be better than mine so that's why I didn't want you to read mine until you hopefully had some fun on the cruise. Keep in mind I didn't have a bad time, but what I wrote in my journal for those days was incredibly, as you would say, lame. I almost tore out the pages, but decided against it.

Any way I'm guessing you'll be docking tomorrow. When you come to the port, follow the directions to town and then the map to an old castle. Make sure it's the right castle!!! After all you are in Ireland and you'll soon see there are many castles. You'll read about my experience at this castle in my journal on your first night there.

A couple there named Edmond and Ellie live there, at least they did when I wrote this. Tell them you're my girl and they'll hook you up for a night or two. Oh, one more thing, buy some rubber boots you're going to need them. Now don't worry about me, go have fun, hopefully it's actually some more fun, because you have already been having fun.

Hugs,
Mom

Famous sat back on the bed, she had planned on staying in and reading her new book. Now she wasn't so sure, there was a knock on the door. "Hey Famous, there's a bunch of us getting together, it's kind of against the rules, but you want to hang with us?"

"Gee, Kai, that sounds great. When and where?"

"We have a crew area, Alex or I will come get you in an hour or so after dinner service so between nine and ten."

She forgot they had to work. Her first thought was about how late it was going to be, "Sounds great see you then." Her thoughts quickly changed to, you only live once.

Famous decided to dress casual, she didn't want to wear the same dress and didn't want or need another one. She ran down and grabbed a bite to eat thinking she didn't feel like going to the main dining area tonight. She walked around the deck and watched the sunset. It was absolutely stunning, she thought about all the sunsets she had missed because she was too busy with her face in a book. This trip had been a gift from her mother.

It was nearly nine when she made it back to her cabin. She brushed her windblown hair and touched up her mascara. Kai and Alex got there just a little later. "Hey there, are you ready?"

"Definitely." They walked down the corridors towards the aft section of the ship. Then down several flights of stairs until they walked into a recreation type area. There were several crew members hanging out. Kai offered her a drink, but she declined. "I don't really drink."

"Cool, there's a lot of us who do the acrobatics and pool shows that don't drink, how about a soda?" Famous grabbed a lemon lime soda and followed Kai. They sat with a group and listened to the chatter for a few minutes before he leaned over and asked. "So what's up with this quest you mentioned last night?"

"Oh, it's a long story," she smiled, "And it keeps getting longer."

"I have all night, there's nothing like a good story."

Alex came over and joined them, "Glad you could make it Famous. It's pretty rare we would bring passengers down, but you seem cool. This is the depths of the boat, no passengers see. We call it crew city, so what are you two talking about?"

"Famous was getting ready to tell me a story." They both sat there looking at her waiting. Famous began the story with her mother's death and the journals. She skipped a lot of unnecessary information and told them of the journey so far and the reason she was going to Ireland. By the time she had finished she had an audience. "Wow, you should write a book."

"Actually, funny thing, Kai, I have written several children's books about a princess on all of these adventures. I never imagined in a million years that I would live them." It had been a pleasant evening, Famous had never felt like one of the crowd before. It was nearly one in the morning before she said she needed to turn in. The next day was probably going to be a long day of travel.

Kai walked her back to her cabin and said goodnight. He handed her a piece of paper with his email address on it. "I'd like to keep in touch, maybe I will see you again sometime."

"That would be nice." She watched as he started to walk away, "Hey thanks for tonight, Kai."

"Sure thing, it was great, you sure are an interesting person Famous. I hope get to see you again real soon." Famous closed the door, it was such a great night. She wrote down every detail in her journal before laying down to get some sleep.

CHAPTER TWENTY THREE

WITCH CASTLE

Famous knew it was going to be a busy day. She needed to get packed and be ready when they got to port. The only thought in her head was coffee. She decided there was nothing in the world so important that couldn't wait an hour. The breakfast buffet was all set up as it had been the previous days. Several of the crew members from the previous night smiled and waved. Some simply told her good morning. Famous felt great, she wished she was staying on the ship longer.

After her much needed coffee and a little breakfast she went back to her cabin and finished up with her packing. She put the journal in the Ziploc bag opened to the page with the directions in the front pocket of her backpack. Then joined the other passengers out on deck. She watched as they approached the docking area, tied the lines and readied the ship for passengers to disembark.

Some passengers would only spend the day and would return for another destination. This was her only and final stop. She stood on deck until she saw passengers walking down the gangplank before making her way toward the exit. Alex and Kai were at the exit to say goodbye, Kai reminded her to email him. They gave her a quick hug and she was off.

It was raining and pretty cool out so she caught a shuttle into town. The scenery was a beautiful blanket of green. In the distance she saw a castle, one of many she was sure she would see over the coming days. Once she made it to the little village, the beginning point of her mother's map, she set out to find some rubber boots and a rain coat.

After a little shopping it was nearly lunch time so she stopped off at a café for a nibble. She sat down and couldn't believe her eyes, the napkin on the table was identical to the one her mom had left! While she was waiting for her food she took out the map and studied it. It didn't look like it was more than three miles away, a very walkable distance.

The waitress was super sweet, she took the time to chat with Famous every time she came to the table. She asked Famous about her visit, how long she'd be in town, who she was visiting, and such.

Famous thought she had nothing to lose and asked, "It seems like a small town, do you by chance know Edmond and Ellie?"

"Edmond and Ellie, yeah sure they're great. They live in the second castle you'll see as you walk down the main road. They run a BNB/hostel, do you know them or did you book it online?"

"Oh well, my mom stayed there about twenty-five years ago so they know my mom. I'm not sure if they are expecting me or not. I hope they have room."

"Believe me they'll make room even if they don't have one. Lovely couple they are. Can I bring you anything else?" Famous shook her head and thanked her. She paid her bill and waved goodbye as she walked out the door.

"The road was dirt, well more like mud, she sloshed along the side for an hour when the rain started to really come down. She had her backpack on under the raincoat so it was dry, but not much else was. There was a castle-like or remnant of a castle-like structure with a for sale sign in front. Famous ran to it to get under cover. She banged on the door, but was pretty sure it was deserted. The big heavy door creaked as she opened it. Inside the door was a large room that still seemed to have a roof. There were furnishings so Famous thought maybe it wasn't abandoned after all. Just as she turned to go back out the door, a voice startled her from behind.

"May I help you?"

Famous turned and started to stutter, "I... I...I... I'm sorry I thought it was abandoned! I was just trying to get out of the rain."

"You should have knocked." The woman was old and looked like one of those witches in a fairytale.

Famous couldn't tell if her words were angry or just a matter of fact. "I did, but, I'm sorry, I'll go."

"Well, you're here already, so the damage is done now, isn't it."

"I guess, um I should really be going, again I'm so sorry."

"Don't be ridiculous you silly child, come have some tea." Famous couldn't explain it, but she was scared of this old woman. "Come into the kitchen." She was practically demanding it. Then Famous looked back at the door and saw herself fleeing for her life. "Well don't just stand there, the kitchen is this way."

Famous reluctantly followed the old woman. She pointed at the table, "Sit." Famous did as she was told and watched her put a kettle on to boil. "You're American," Famous nodded. "This is not exactly a tourist area, why are you here?" She sounded meaner by the minute. Famous tried to calm herself, telling herself that she's just an old woman and she was being silly. Famous looked back towards the room with the front door, thinking maybe she should make a run for it. When she turned back she could swear the old woman was sprinkling some powder in her tea.

"I should go, I'm supposed to be somewhere." Famous was thinking, anywhere, but here. "So thank you, but I've got to go."

The old woman looked back at her from the stove, "Sit down, Famous."

Her eyes got really wide, "How did you know my name?" She was backing toward the door now. "I didn't tell you my name and don't try saying that it was a lucky guess because that never applies to my name."

"I know a lot about you. I've been expecting you for many years now."

Famous was putting on her raincoat, "Expecting me? Well I don't know anything about you and I think I need to be going now!"

"Don't be frightened child, I won't hurt you. Your mother is a lovely woman she stopped here many years ago."

"My mother was a lovely woman, she passed away, so you don't know so much."

"Maybe it's you, who doesn't know so much."

"What's that supposed to mean?"

"Your mother still lives, maybe just not in the same sense that you do. Now let's take off that coat and have some tea."

"I think I'll pass on that tea." Famous started to get more and more nervous. "I think I'll be going now." She started to walk out of the kitchen. She was looking back at the kitchen, but when she turned around to open the door the old woman was in front of it. "Please, I must go now." Famous was frantic when there was a banging on the door. The old woman seemed to ignore it. Famous yelled "Come in, I'm in here, please come in."

The door creaked open and a beautiful woman appeared in the doorway. There was a man standing right behind her. "Famous?"

"How does everyone know my name?"

"I'm sorry, who is everyone?"

"Well the old woman," she glanced around and there was no one there.

"What old woman? We received a phone call from the gal at the café in town and when you didn't show up, I got worried so we came looking for you. When we didn't find you on the road we figured you must have come into this place to get out of the rain. It's been abandoned for years."

"Abandoned, it's not abandoned, there's an old woman here."

"Famous you must be tired, there hasn't been anyone here for years. You must have fallen asleep and had a dream. We've looked for you for hours."

Famous interrupted her, "Hours? No I was here only for a few minutes"

Ellie smiled, "Well never mind, anyway, I am Ellie, and this is Edmond, it's so wonderful to see you. Come let's go, we have a room all set up for you."

Famous looked back toward the kitchen and around the room. It looked different somehow, but she didn't know how. She felt confused, "It was real, I'm sure of it. There was an old woman, you must believe me!"

Ellie took her hand, "Let's go get you by the fire, you must be freezing." She led Famous out the door. They sloshed through the mud and down the road until they came to their castle. Famous followed Ellie inside where there was a warm glow from the fire. "That place is a little creepy, huh?"

"That's an understatement, and I think haunted too. So you're saying no one lives there and you're sure of that?"

"Not for many years, you're not the only one who says they saw an old woman there though."

"Why did you act like I was crazy?"

"I thought it best to get you out of there as quickly as possible. We have heard some things about that place."

"Like what?"

"It makes no never mind." Ellie helped Famous off with her coat. "Let me show you your room, you can put your backpack in there. And get changed out of those wet clothes. Are you hungry? Dinner is a couple of hours away, but I'd be happy to fix you a snack and maybe some tea."

In a stern panicky voice Famous screeched, "Definitely no tea, I don't want any tea." Famous looked around, she was feeling nervous. Ellie could tell she was really shaken and placed her hand on Famous. Famous felt the warmth and kindness of the gesture. "I'm sorry, I must sound like a real loon to you."

"Not at all, I'm sure you have had quite an experience these last few days. After we take your things to your room you should tell us all about it. I remember when your mother came here. It was such a different world then. I can hardly wait to share stories with you. So much to talk about and…"

Edmond interrupted her, "Ellie, let the poor girl relax a minute." He took Famous' backpack, "Let me show to your room." Famous followed Edmond up the narrow, winding staircase, it was small and reminded Famous of a corkscrew. Ellie followed right behind prattling on about Dar and when she was here this and when she was here that. Edmond finally told her to hush for a minute, and said there would be plenty of time for talking later. They came to a landing that opened into a large room with a bed, armoire, and a nightstand. "Here we are, I hope you like it."

"It's lovely, thank you." The room was bright and full of color, especially for a castle, Famous thought. The stone walls had been painted a faint color of yellow. The bed cover had oranges, yellows, and greens. Every bit of décor was carefully chosen to brighten the room. It gave Famous a feeling of happiness.

"Every room in the castle has a name, this is the sunshine room. Maybe later we can show you the other rooms that are vacant. You have your own bathroom just through that door." She pointed to a small door Famous had originally thought was probably a closet. "Anyway we will let you get settled, or get some rest. Whatever you need, come down when

you'd like. Oh I blocked off this room from our website for a few days, but being Dar's daughter you can stay as long as you like. At no charge of course." Ellie beamed as she said her mother's   name.
"Oh no, I should definitely pay for the room."

"Don't be ridiculous you are practically family. I am so thrilled you are here. All the times your mother came and all the letters, it's just so good to see you in person." Ellie was holding her shoulders looking at her and hugged her tight.

Edmund's Irish accent was strong, Famous struggled to understand him. "Okay Ellie, let the poor girl get situated, we need to get things started for dinner. You come down whenever you want. Take all the time you need." Edmond ushered Ellie out the door.

Famous went to investigate the bathroom. It was a brighter color of yellow. There was a claw foot bathtub and shower nozzle. No shower curtain, her mom had once told her that many bathrooms in Europe didn't seem to have shower curtains. She pulled her hair back in a ponytail and washed her face. Looking in the mirror, she splashed her face with cold water again. She could not get the events from earlier out of her head. It was real, she knew it had to be real. How had she lost hours of time?

She was thinking that maybe tomorrow she would go back to investigate, but that sent a chill down her back.

Famous busied herself with unpacking to try to push those thoughts from her head. She sat and wrote in her journal and thought about reading more from her mother's. Then changed her mind and decided that she could wait until bedtime. She wanted to visit with this lovely couple that were friends of her mother before she was her mother.

CHAPTER TWENTY FOUR

EVERYONE COMES WITH A STORY

Famous started down the stairs, as she was approaching the bottom step she overheard Ellie talking about the witch that haunts the castle down the road. When Famous entered the room she stopped talking. "So there was a witch?" Famous was looking at them waiting for an answer.

"It's a long story, I was just going in to make dinner."

"Want some help? I'd love to hear some stories about my mom and then maybe you can tell me this long story about the witch."

"Sure, I guess it's inevitable after what you saw today." Edmond followed behind them as they walked in the kitchen. Ellie pulled a bunch of vegetables from the fridge while Edmond started cooking some sausage. Famous and Ellie were cleaning and cutting the vegetables when Ellie began her story. "It's really just supposed to be a fable, but they have tried to sell that property for so long. According to the rumors, several people that go in to look at that place, encounter this little old woman. Sometimes she is pleasant while at other times she scares them to near death. Regardless, we have been hearing stories for over twenty years. So there are several versions, like I said a long story."

Ellie started to prepare some garlic cheese bread to go with dinner. "You know let's come back to this later it will take a lot of time, besides wouldn't you rather talk about your mom?" Famous smiled and nodded her head. "So your mom got off the ship, the same as you. Obviously you haven't read her journal from the ship to here. You can read about that later, but did you know she went to the same café as you?"

"Yeah, she left a napkin with her journals from there."

"Your mom, she was amazing, she talked about you like she already had you. She stayed here a few days, they told her about our place at the café. You see back then they didn't exactly have the internet so the town folks were good about helping us get renters. We also had the occasional hikers that we let stay free. It was a different time."

A couple walked in the kitchen asking Ellie what time dinner was going to be served? Edmond and Ellie chatted with them. Famous watched Ellie as she was adding vegetables to the meat, making a marinara sauce.

Then looked around the room, the walls and the floors were stone. It was what you would envision when you think of a castle. Many things had been added since it was built, there was a big stove Edmond had loaded wood into. The cabinets were white armoire type. Famous was thinking when this place was built they didn't build a kitchen like they do now. She listened to the couple mention some places they had been to and asked about other tourist type of things they should see and do while in Ireland.

Ellie glanced over at Famous, "Oh, I'm so sorry, I'm being terribly rude. Where are my manners? Famous, these are two of our guests Jarod and Suzy. Jarod, Suzy this is Famous." They said hello and commented on her name as everyone did. "Her mom was a very dear friend of ours and a little eccentric."

They chatted back and forth for few minutes before Ellie asked Famous if she would set the table for seven as the two other guests had said that they would be back by dinner. Suzy helped Famous get the table set.

They chatted about Suzy and Jarod's vacation. Suzy asked Famous if she had only come to see Ellie and Edmond. She told her a short version of her reason for the trip.

"Wow that sounds so interesting. So you really just got on a train?"

Famous beamed with pride, "Yep and believe me, that's not in my character. I'm not the free spirit my mom was. It has definitely been an interesting couple of weeks."

Suzy was entranced, "I'd love to hear all about it as it sounds so exciting!"

"Me too," Ellie said as she walked in the room. "I remember when your mom came, the stories she told of her journey up to that point were so colorful. I could listen to her talk for hours. Anyway dinner is about done, any sign of the guys?" She heard the front door open, "I guess that must be them."

Edmond brought the spaghetti, while Jarod followed with the salad and garlic bread. Famous looked at the table, it made her think of those movies where families would get together at dinner time. They would sit around the table to eat and talk about their day. It has always been just her and her mom.

It was random, her and her mom would sit around in the front room to chat about the day, type of eating sessions. Famous had never had the big family dinners, not that she felt like she missed anything. She loved the way food had become a bonding time for her and her mother. They cooked, they baked, and they ate together all the time. Famous thought it was just a different form of a big family dinner.

Edmond was standing in the doorway when two young guys walked in. They both had long hair, one looked like he had dreadlocks, pulled back while the other had it pulled up in a bun. "Famous this is Mike and Jack. They are on a hiking trip they started in Scotland and you will find their story is interesting as well. They take free rides to where ever the people are going. Then they find odd jobs for a room and food. It's really much more interesting when they tell it."

"Oh wow, that sounds super interesting. How long have you been on your trip? How long do you plan to continue?"

Mike shrugged, "Not really sure, we're hoping to make it to Africa in at least a year time frame. We have nothing but time for an adventure."

"Yeah, Mike and I got this great idea about six months ago. We worked day in and day out saving every penny. We set a goal date of departure no matter how much money we had saved, we were going to make it work. We left six weeks ago and what a ride it's been. We haven't even really spent hardly any money so far, we actually earned a little."

Famous was hanging on his every word. "I was amazed at how little I've spent, but I've only been on my journey for a short time. I didn't plan my trip at all."

"So one day you just decided to go, and went? That's awesome, you need to tell us that story. Like Jarod said it's been a ride, we have met so many people and heard so many stories. We take turns writing in a journal, maybe someday we will co-author on a book or something."

"I keep a journal too, actually, believe it or not it was a journal that started my journey."

Ellie brought some salad dressings and parmesan cheese and set them on the table. "Well, I see everyone is getting acquainted. I hate to interrupt, but dinner is getting cold. So take a seat and let's eat!" Everyone laughed at her rhyme.

Famous said, "Ellie, Edmond, your dinner is excellent, thank you so much." Which caused a round of comments of appreciation and compliments from the other members at the table. "So Mike, how long are you guys here for?"

"No idea, we caught a ride on a boat over and have been traveling south with various people. When we got here we saw the Edmonds flier at the market asking for help chopping wood for the winter. We couldn't pass up the free food and lodging. We will stay until we go, ha-ha, or until they don't need our help anymore."

"Yeah it's so funny, Mike and I didn't even plan on coming to Ireland. We were hitching rides and planned to go south through the UK when a guy stopped and asked us where we were headed. Then after we shrugged, he asked if we wanted to help out on a fishing boat for a couple of days that was headed for Ireland. We earned a few quid and they had some decent food on board. We are just taking it as it comes. What about you Famous?"

"I'm following a path of specific places that my mother followed to where she found me."

"Found you?"

"Found me, that's what I meant earlier, it's my mother's journals that started my journey." That brought about a bunch of questions. Ellie suggested they clear the table and that Famous should tell her story from the beginning in the bean bag room around a nice big fire. Everyone pitched in cleaning the dishes, anxiously waiting to hear the story of Famous. Ellie prepared some hot chocolate and a tray with the makings for s'mores.

It was cozy in the bean bag room. Bean bags were strewn about the floor on a large area rug, there was no other furniture in the room. Three of the walls were shelves and shelves of books. Books of many different genres and in many different languages. Famous thought back to the library, she walked down the walls touching various books. She had read some of the books, but had never heard of many of them. She pictured her mother here reading by the fire. It was her mother's love of books that gave her the same love. She had read to her and told her stories throughout her whole life.

When she reached the fourth wall it was nearly covered in pictures. They were organized by years, Ellie walked up and pointed at pictures of her mother. There she was smiling with her face buried in a book, drinking hot chocolate, or just lying by the fire. "There are more of her with you when she was on her way back to the states down here." She pointed at the pictures. Her eyes filled with tears as she saw her mother holding her with so much love. Her smile melted Famous' heart. "You can see the love she had for you."

"I didn't know she brought me here." Ellie had her arm around her shoulder.

"The two of you stayed for over a month. It was a magical time for your mother, and for you." Famous looked at picture after picture. "Everyone is waiting for us by the fire. You can stay here as long as you want, we have plenty of time to talk and look at these pictures."

Famous hugged her tight and whispered, "Thank you." Ellie hugged her for a few minutes and could feel how much she missed her. She wiped the tears from her cheeks and with a smile and led Famous over to join the group. She sat in front of the fire and told the story. Although it had begun a short time ago it felt like so much had happened. As she told the story it was like she couldn't believe it was her that she was talking about.

The group talked until late in the evening. Ellie took a bunch of pictures for her picture wall. She said that she was worried she would soon run out of room and have to find another wall. She thought probably in the dining room. Famous could see why her mother loved it here. From the moment she had gotten here she felt warmth and love. Finally they all started to turn in for the evening. As Famous climbed the stairs she thought about the night. It had gone completely different than she had hoped, but turned out better than she could have ever wished.

CHAPTER TWENTY FIVE

TEA TIME WITH THE PRINCESS

Famous brushed her teeth and changed into her pajamas. She had to dig out her warm socks because castles are a little drafty. She opened her mother's journal to the page where the map and directions were. She flipped to the next page and began to read.

Today I reached the port in Ireland. I caught a ride to the local town. I came to a café where I could get some coffee and a snack. The waitress was in a chatty mood, she asked me about my visit to their small town. I asked her about a hotel and she told me about a local couple that had been renovating a castle. She said I could stay there cheap. I stuffed one of their napkins in my purse so I could show them who gave me their information. After adding a map with the directions she gave me in my journal. So I wouldn't lose them and I was on my way.

The mud path that she called a road was a mess, I wished I had thought to buy some rubber boots. I walked for an hour and came to a castle, it looked a lot more run down than I had imagined, but I knocked on the big wooden door. Several minutes had gone by and no one came to the door. I knocked again when the door creaked open there was an old woman. She invited me in, I looked around and it didn't look like it was being renovated at all.

I asked if this was Ellie and Edmonds place. The old woman just beckoned me to come in and have some tea. Something about the situation seemed off. I told her I had to go, but she was so insistent that I followed her into the kitchen. I watched her as she made tea. I started to get up but she told me to sit. I couldn't believe I was scared of this little old woman, but I was. Her hands shook as she set the cup in front of me. She sat across from me just staring at me. Now I must say it gave me the creeps for sure. She told me to drink, in a manner that made me definitely not want to drink the tea.

I stood up and grabbed my bag when I felt this cold hand on my shoulder shove me back in the chair. I looked at her, she had not moved. Now I was freaking out. I tried to get up, but it felt like I was being held in place. She again told me to drink my tea, but I declined and told her that I needed to leave. She told me that I wasn't leaving until she was ready for me to leave.

I guess it was about this time I started to panic. I squirmed in the chair trying with all my might to get up. I was unsuccessful, so I drank the tea, what else could I do? Now this is where I am using my best recollection of the events that followed. After my first sip I was very relaxed. The old woman seemed to fade to a young *beautiful woman. I rubbed my eyes in disbelief. She had long golden red hair and beautiful green eyes. I was so confused it was like a dream.*

Famous was getting so sleepy she was having a hard time reading. Her eyes kept closing and she would drift off only to force herself awake again. She read a few more words and finally lost the battle into dreamland. Famous dreamt of the creepy old woman turning to a beautiful young woman, then she turned into a witch. The witch was holding her poor mother hostage. Famous sat straight up, her heart was racing.

She picked the journal back up and started reading. She reread the last couple of paragraphs and started to drift off to sleep again. Finally she gave up and set the journal on the nightstand. She shut off the light and tried to go back to sleep. Her mind was racing back to her mother's words. It was useless, she turned the lamp back on, got a glass of water and began reading again. She started where she had left off.

I was so confused it was like a dream. I could hear her talking to me, but couldn't make out the words. It seemed like she was telling me a story, I tried to focus and listen to what she was saying. It was blurry or I was blurry. I kept saying what, or I don't understand, and asking her to start over. Finally everything became clearer, she asked me if I understood her now. I just nodded and started to take another sip of the tea, but she stopped me. She said I had had enough for now and gave me a glass of water.

Suddenly everything came into focus. She was beautiful, no longer an old woman, no longer a scary witch. She began her story by telling me her name was Angelica and how she had once been a princess, but only for a day. Her family was exiled with rumors of her being a witch. It wasn't that she was a witch, magical things just seemed to happen in her life. Animals flocked to her, she was the most beautiful woman in the land, and she was blessed in every way. A truly blissful life of happiness. Everything fell into place for her until the day when she was crowned the princess of the land.

A real witch was so jealous of her beauty and the way she was so loved by all of the people in the land. She put a curse on Angelica, then publically accused her of being a witch. The curse made her appear as a witch and doomed her existence in that castle in life and death.

The people of the land were afraid of witches so they went to confront her. When the people of the land looked at her they now saw a witch. It became a witch hunt where she was the hunted. Her family had lived in this grand castle, the grandest in the land at the time. What once was her home was now her prison.

She tried to hide when they came to her castle again only this time with torches. She was not a witch, but something changed that night. She knew they were burning so-called witches at the stake. When they stormed her castle and found her they shackled her in the cellar. She fought and screamed and even cried. Her fiery death sealed her fate, she was now trapped in this castle for all of eternity.

She went on to say that only the pure of heart can see her beauty with her special tea. So every time someone comes she tries to make them drink the tea. I was the first one in all of this time that was able to hear her story. I felt a deep sadness and wished there was a way I could help her. She was so alone and longed for someone to keep her company even if only for a little while. I told her about my journey to find my precious little girl. As time went on I suddenly felt very sleepy, I could not keep my eyes open any longer.

I was awakened by drops of rain on my face. When I open my eyes I was outside of the castle door. I rubbed my eyes and wondered if it had all been just a dream. I knocked on the door over and over again, she wouldn't answer. I tried to open the door but it was locked. It was getting late so I decided to find Ellie and Edmond's castle.

Famous closed the journal, she sat back on the bed trying to process what she had just read. It all seemed so unbelievable she just didn't know what to think. Famous was so tired, it was late so she decided to get some rest. As she laid there her mind was racing. She could only think of this poor woman's story of being turned into a witch. She couldn't imagine being trapped for all of eternity. Although it was hard to believe she knew that she had seen her earlier that day. When she finally fell asleep she had dreams of the beautiful princess that she once was.

CHAPTER TWENTY SIX

Picture This

Famous woke up with thoughts of what she had read in her mother's journal. Famous got out her own journal and wrote about the previous day. She wrote about the dinner, her new friends, and the pictures on the wall. Thinking of coffee, as she ran down the stairs and found Ellie curled up in the beanbag room drinking coffee and reading a book. "Good morning Famous how did you sleep?"

"Well it was interesting, I read my mother's journal until I fell asleep. Then I had a nightmare and couldn't sleep and so I continued to read about my mother's experience in the castle down the road. It seemed like such an incredible story. I'm guessing that's why you put off telling me so I could read it for myself."

"Yes, I felt it would be better coming from your mother. It was quite a story I remember the day she told me, like it was yesterday."

Famous sat down in a beanbag next to Ellie. "Did you ever go over there?"

"Funny thing, I have started to a million times but just can never bring myself to go there. Your mother was a special and wonderful woman with the purest heart of anyone I've ever known. I guess in some way I fear my heart is not as pure. I know it is silly but sometimes I think about Dar and am in awe of the person she was."

"I get that, I wonder what would have happened if I had drank the tea. I'm still curious about how she knew my name, but I guess it doesn't matter."

Ellie got up to get some more coffee, "Would you like some coffee?"

"Definitely," Famous followed her into the kitchen. "It's kind of quiet, where is everyone?"

"The guys are out chopping wood. I think that Suzy went into town to do some shopping. She and Jarod were going to leave today and go to Dublin but had decided to stay on another day or so. So Jarod is helping Edmond, Mike, and Jack in return for the room. Which is really great because we got a late start this year. We will need a lot of wood for the winter. I'm not sure if Edmond asked Jarod or vice versa but I'm really grateful." Ellie poured them each a cup of coffee and pointed to the sugar.

Famous and Ellie went back into the beanbag room to chat. "I have so many questions. I don't even know where to start. I didn't realize how much time my mother had spent here and apparently me too. So my mother has kept in contact with you all these years?"

"She sent me letters nearly every month of your life. I have a few photo walls in other rooms. One is of just you and Dar, just my favorite pictures, the rest are in albums. The photos on the wall in the bean bag room are only the ones taken here. I can show you the photo albums if you'd like."

"That would be lovely, I would like that very much." Ellie left the room for a minute and came back with three photo albums. They flipped through the pages of her life for over an hour before Ellie insisted on making them some breakfast. Famous went with her to help her prepare breakfast. When Famous started cooking bacon her stomach growled. "I guess I am hungry."

Ellie made some potatoes and eggs while Famous cooked bacon and toasted some English muffins. When they were finished Famous set the table while Ellie was out getting the boys to come in and eat. Everyone sat at the table and they were so hungry not a word was said. Ellie told Famous that the secret to everyone loving your cooking is making sure they are near starvation when you serve it.

Famous helped Ellie with the cleanup and the guys went back outside. "Ellie?"

"Hmm?"

"I was thinking, well, what do you think about you and me going to that castle together?"

"Oh gee, Famous, I don't know if that is a good idea. I mean I've never heard of anyone getting hurt or anything. Several times I've heard of people leaving there so completely terrified. I don't know if I am prepared to do that."

"Will you at least think about it? I'm thinking I might want to go there before I leave. Then of course I was thinking I might leave tomorrow so today would be my only chance. Well I guess I could stop on my way back but I feel like I want to get going soon."

"I thought you were going to stay for a few more days. I really do hope that you will come back before you go back to the States."

"I just feel like I have so much more of a journey and I can't stay away from home forever. I'm not even sure how much longer this journey will take me. How long was my mom gone?"

"I would rather not say because although you're following her journey to finding you, you must have your own journey as well. I understand if you feel like you must go and maybe when you come back I will consider going to that castle with you. I just need some time to think about it so I'm not sure that I could do that today."

They finished with the cleanup and went back into the beanbag room. Ellie took her to the wall of pictures and started telling her stories for each of the pictures on the wall. They spent hours talking about her mother and looking at the pictures. Famous had always been close to her mother, but this was a side of her that she did not know. Ellie looked at the time and said she needed to run into town and get a few things for dinner and asked if Famous would like to go. Famous said she was going to go up to take a shower.

Ellie grabbed her purse and left for the store. Famous climbed the stairs to her room. When she got to her room she decided to read another letter from her mother. She sat down on the bed and pulled the pack of letters from the drawer in the night stand. Famous opened the fifth letter and a picture of her and her mother with flour on their face and in their hair fell out. She remembered the day and immediately it made her smile. She remembers her mother taking that picture. She closed her eyes and thought back to that day. Famous visualized them in the kitchen laughing and laughing. She opened her eyes and began to read.

Famous,

If you haven't already, take a look at the picture. What a day we had today, probably the best baking day ever! Right now you are on your way to take our baked goods to the homeless shelter. I'm just so exhausted and so sorry that I didn't go with you. Sometimes I picture you reading my letters and hope that they bring you joy. I know sometimes they will give you sadness and I'm sorry for that.

It was so funny today when we got into that flour fight. I hope when you think of me, these are the times that you remember the most. I know it'll be hard for a few months, but I hope that this journey helps you to heal and to find yourself. I want to have days like this every day if it is possible.

I am so sorry that at this time I still have been unable to tell you the truth. I guess I'm afraid that you will be different. I think that it has changed me, but I'm trying to not dwell on the sadness. I want what time I have left to be special. I've been thinking that maybe you and I should take a trip. So I will talk about that with you soon. You have always been the reason for my existence. I was born to find you. I hope I have always been the mother you would have chosen. I just heard your car in the driveway so I must close for now.

Love,
Mom

She couldn't stop the tears, she hugged her legs close, and buried her face in her knees and cried. She kept saying how it was so unfair and why her. Famous put the letter back in the envelope. She went to the bathroom to take a shower. Tears were streaming down her face harder as the hot water rained down on her head. She knew her mother was trying to help her, but sometimes it made it harder. Her mother wanted her to face, and deal with the hurt she was feeling rather than hide in the library or a book. Which is exactly what she had done for seven long years.

She closed her eyes and thought back to the picture. She smiled and remembered baking bread, cookies, and cupcakes that day. She was standing with a mixing bowl in her hand. She remembered turning to ask her mother a question. She didn't think about it then, but now she remembers that she looked like she was in pain. Before Famous could say anything, her mother threw flour in her face. Famous retaliated and threw some back. They made a huge mess and ended up sitting on the kitchen floor laughing and laughing.

After her shower Famous put the letter away and put the pack of letters back in the nightstand. She picked up her mother's journal and turned the page.

When I found Ellie and Edmonds place they welcomed me and took me to the sunshine room. The room was so bright and lovely, I felt warm and happy.

Famous looked around the room and thought of her sitting in the very same place. It made her feel happy too. She imagined her sitting next to her telling her a story.

I followed them back downstairs and helped prepare dinner. While we were cooking I told Ellie what had happened earlier at the other castle. I'm not sure if she believed me or if she thought I was crazy. She did say that she had heard stories that old place was haunted. The rest of the night after dinner we sat around in the beanbag room and talked about our adventures. Ellie took pictures of all of us. She said she was going to start a wall of pictures.

There was ten of us there tonight. One I became instant friends with was Johnathon. He believed my story, he was there investigating undocumented witch trials and haunted castles. He went to the castle many times. He had some weird pictures, and stories of the old woman, but he never drank the tea. He asked me dozens of questions. Now he wished he had drank the tea, but I'm not sure because you have to have a pure heart to see her. Otherwise, it could be a terrifying visit.

What a great place, I'm so glad that waitress told me about it. I think though, I will be leaving in the next day or so because I feel I need to move on. I must find my baby girl. I dream of her nearly every night now. I wonder if that means I'm getting closer. I am undecided if I will go back to that castle again before I leave. I guess I should get some sleep for tomorrow's another day.

CHAPTER TWENTY SEVEN

A LITTLE CRAZY

Famous turned the page, there was a note from her mom. It said not to read on until she was ready to leave Ellie and Edmond's. The journal snapped closed. She thought it was curious that it didn't happen every time. She placed in on the nightstand and headed downstairs.

The guys were coming in to take showers and Ellie was in the kitchen. When Famous walked in, Ellie was singing a song. Famous smiled and thought back to all the times she walked in and caught her mother singing in the kitchen.

"How was your shower?"

Famous didn't want to talk about her small breakdown. She smiled, "It was good. How was your shopping?"

"Oh you know, I found stuff and bought it?" They both smiled.

The night went by pretty quickly, it was much the same as the previous night. They ended up in the beanbag room telling stories. Ellie prodded Famous to tell about her mother's experience at the castle. Everyone sat in disbelief. Then she told of her own experience and how Ellie and Edmond had gotten there before she drank the tea.

At the end of the evening Famous told everyone she would be leaving in the morning. They were all sad and wishing she would stay longer. She explained she had to get back on the road, but she would be back soon. At least she hoped so.

"We will have a big good bye breakfast in the morning. I can't have you leaving on an empty stomach, can I? No proper Irish woman would!"

Famous hugged her, "Thank you, that's so sweet."

Everyone turned in for the night. Famous wrote a quick note in her journal about her day. Famous laid down in bed and thought about her next trek. She wondered where she would be going. Her eyes were heavy as she drifted off to sleep.

Before she knew it, it was morning. Famous slept good, it was the most restful night of sleep she had had in a long time. It was still early so she began packing her things in her backpack. That was one thing she really liked about packing so lightly, she could be packed and ready in no time. She got in the shower and got ready to continue on with her journey. She opened her mother's journal and read the next page.

I had to say goodbye today it was harder than I thought it would be. We had a big breakfast, everyone was so kind to me. Ellie drove me to town this morning so I could take a bus to Dublin. The bus ride was pleasant enough, I enjoyed watching the scenery. Ireland is so beautiful and green, it rained every day but I guess it would have to, to stay so beautiful. I stayed in a hostel in Dublin for the night.

There was a note for her at the bottom of the page that said:

Famous I hope you have had a wonderful visit with Ellie, Edmond, and whoever else might have been there. Travel safely now to Dublin and when you get there enjoy the evening. Do some sightseeing, maybe you can find a library and look up the history of that castle. I know that is something you will enjoy. Well that's all for now, read on in Dublin at bedtime for your next destination, love mom.

Famous could hear some noises coming from downstairs. She grabbed her backpack, took one more look around, and headed down the stairs. Ellie and Suzy were in the kitchen.

They were pulling things out of the fridge for breakfast. "Good morning girls, what can I do to help?"

"Not a thing, this morning's breakfast is in your honor. You just sit down and relax. I will get you some coffee."

"I love coffee, but I'll feel like a lazy bum if I don't do something to help."

Ellie brought her some oranges, a cutting board, and a knife. "If you can cut these up that would be great. Here's a bowl for the center of the table." Famous cut the oranges and drank her coffee. She listened to Suzy and Ellie talk about Suzy's shopping trip.

Suzy asked Famous where she was heading. She told her that she was going to Dublin. "Really, Dublin? Jarod and I are going there this morning, we can give you a ride if you like."

"That would be great, are you sure?"

"Absolutely, we were going to stay another night and skip Dublin. But Ellie said we would be silly to come all the way to Ireland and miss seeing Dublin."

"It looks like this breakfast should be in your honor as well." Famous was so happy she would get to Dublin early enough to go to the library. She would have to get a new sim card for her phone. She wanted to be able to check her email, email Kai from the ship, and could use Google to get around.

Ellie poured more coffee in Famous' cup and brought her the sugar dish. "You look like you're deep in thought."

"I'm just making plans in my head. I probably think way too much. I'm trying to live in the minute, but it's genuinely a challenge for me. Thank you, this coffee is great, what's your secret?"

"I grated fresh nutmeg on the grounds before I brewed it. Sometimes I use cinnamon, sometimes orange zest, just whatever I'm in the mood for."

"What a great tip, thanks. Breakfast smells so delicious."

"Make your own breakfast burritos are always a big hit. Famous would you like to cut up some fresh tomatoes and onions?"

"Sure thing." Famous grabbed everything she needed and took it back to the table so she could stay out of the way while Suzy and Ellie buzzed about the kitchen. "Ellie, do you know who owns that old castle?"

"No one has lived there since we've been here. It might be owned by the tax man by now. I bet you could call the number on the for sale sign. Why?"

"I don't know, just something my mom said. I was thinking about trying to find out some of its history when I'm in Dublin, is all. There is an archive library there. If I could find out some information I mean, you know, when I came back, oh never mind it's probably a silly thought."

"What is a silly thought?"

"Well, there must be a way to break the curse, right?"

"Famous, I sometimes wonder if your mom was dreaming. I know your experience and all, but maybe you should just forget about it. At least for now you should focus on your journey."

"Yeah I suppose you're right, but maybe this is part of my journey." Suzy began setting the table and Famous pulled out some juice glasses. "It's just such a sad story, isn't it?"

The guys came in and got washed up. Suzy told Jarod about Famous riding with them to Dublin. They all sat down to eat. Everyone agreed it was an amazing breakfast. Famous was stuffed, she ate way too much. She was holding her stomach and groaning. Ellie laughed and the others joined in. "I should know my limits, but it was so good. No, it was too good, I blame you both." She was looking at Ellie and Suzy. She groaned again.

"Famous we should be ready in about an hour, is that good for you?"

"Sounds good." Famous helped clean the breakfast dishes. She went into the beanbag room and looked at the pictures of her and her mother. They were such happy pictures. She wondered if her mother ever thought about helping Angelica. Maybe she did, maybe she even tried, and Ellie wouldn't talk about it.

Ellie walked in to the room, "She was so happy. You know when she came here before she found you she was so certain of her path. She talked about helping the witch, but she knew you needed her. I don't know how she knew, I can't really explain it. She went back to that castle, did you know that?"

Famous turned from the pictures, "She did, when?"

"Before she went to Dublin. She knocked and knocked and even tried the door. She told me she walked around to see if there was any other way in with no luck."

"She didn't mention it in her journal, at least not as far as I've read."

"She went again when she came back with you."

Famous hadn't noticed that Ellie didn't say what had happened. She just assumed she had no luck and interrupted her. "I was there, I was inside that castle. She was there, she offered me tea."

"Sweetie, I don't have any answers. I do know that you, like your mother, are on a journey and I don't think you can help her. I'm not even sure she wants help, that is, if she even exists."

"Are you even the least bit curious? I mean the castle is right down the road."

"Sometimes, I guess, when I drive past. I don't think about it really. Your mom tried, but she made the choice that you were more important. If Angelica is there and wanted your mom to help her she would have allowed her in. I think it's really that simple."

"Yeah, you're right about that. It has just made me a little crazy." Ellie put her arm around her shoulders, "I'm so glad you're here and I hope you do come back. I think we've had enough of this witch talk."

CHAPTER TWENTY EIGHT

DUBLIN

Famous hugged Ellie and Edmond good bye and climbed into the back seat. "Don't worry I will be back, thank you so much. I can see why my mother loved it here and you both so much. I'm so glad that I was able to come here."

"We are too sweetie and we will be right here waiting to hear about the rest of your journey when you come back."

Suzy and Jarod put their luggage in the trunk and thanked Ellie and Edmond for their hospitality. They promised to try to come back again sometime. After a few more hugs they climbed in the car to get on the road. Famous waved as they drove away. They passed the other castle and Famous just stared at it. She asked Jarod to slow down so she could take down the number. He looked at Suzy and she shrugged. He came to a stop in front of the sign. Famous jotted down the number and thanked Jarod.

They had a nice conversation during the drive. Famous asked about their life, they were from Italy. She told them about her life in New York. She described it as boring especially compared to the last couple of weeks. Suzy told Famous about the places they planned to visit in Dublin. She even invited her to go if she wanted.

"That's so nice, but I am going to go to the library. Maybe we could meet up for dinner. You could message or email me. I'm afraid I haven't gotten a sim card yet. I am really back and forth on it because I'd love to have the internet. It is so much easier to find your way around. Then I think about the fact that I may leave Ireland in a day or two and I'm not sure about the sim card working in multiple countries."

The drive only took about two and a half hours. Famous had them drop her off near the subway. She handed Suzy a paper with her email address on it. "I'm not sure what I'm doing yet, but if I don't see you two tonight I hope you'll keep in touch."

"Definitely, I have to hear about the rest of your trip." Suzy hugged her good bye and wished her luck.

On the drive, Famous had decided she was going to need to get a sim card or find a place with Wi-Fi. Famous found a store close by that sold sim cards. She hated to spend the money, but knew it would make it so much easier to find a hostel or hotel. She also wanted to be able to use a maps app to get around Dublin. She was in awe of the buildings, she saw the Dublin castle and made a mental note to see about taking a tour.

Famous stopped at the park to appreciate the fountain in front of the Great Saint Patrick's Cathedral. As she stood there looking at the construction of these buildings her thoughts went back to the castle. She searched for the Dublin library on her phone. She couldn't believe her search results, there were several. She decided to find a place for the night before she made a decision on which library she would go to. She found a cheap BNB near the city center and headed for the archive library.

The staff was very helpful, she found a lot of books on witches and castles, but couldn't find anything about Angelica. She searched for hours. She even researched curses and witch trials, but that too was of no help. She read that Ireland had a history of fairies and druids, but not a lot of witches. The Irish culture respected their powers and had a significantly lower number of witch trials than nearly every other country. There were only four recorded and estimated that only a few more possibly had happened.

Famous decided she needed to move on. There was nothing more she could learn at this point. She was in one of the most beautiful historical cities she had ever been to. She wasn't going to spend all of her time in a library like she had spent most of her life. First thing she did when she left the library was go check in to her room and drop off her backpack. Her room was small and quaint, but it was also cheap and clean.

Her first thought was a snack, she had missed lunch. Famous headed towards the castle to take a tour. On the way she stopped and grabbed a slice of pizza. When she got to the castle she ran into Suzy and Jarod. They all took the tour together the history amazed Famous. The U.S. is so young in comparison. After the tour they enjoyed a nice meal at a Texas style barbeque restaurant. After dinner they walked around the city for an hour or two together. Famous wanted to call it an early night so she said goodbye and went back to her room for the evening.

She sat down at the little table and wrote about her day's events. She included what she had learned and not learned at the library. She wrote in detail the majesty of the castle and her visit with her new friends. Then she took out her mother's journal to read about her next destination. She opened to the last page she had read. When she flipped the page there was a note stapled in.

Hope you have enjoyed Dublin, I sure did. So tomorrow get on the Dublin ferry to Liverpool. Tonight, buy a plane ticket from Liverpool to Warsaw. It was pretty cheap when I wrote this, I hope it still is. Most of the tickets around Europe are reasonable. While in Liverpool visit the World Museum it's a must see. My friend is located in St. Helens, her name is Julie and her number was on a paper with the napkin, train ticket, and other miscellaneous tokens I left for you. She will put you up for a few nights or whatever you need for your flight to be reasonable.

Famous remembered seeing a paper with a series of numbers and the name Julie printed on the bottom. She dug it out of the bag and called the number, but it was no longer in service. There was no last name, she couldn't just go to this town and ask every woman on the street if their name was Julie so she was going to have to come up with a plan B. Famous booked a ferry for the next day. She found a flight to Warsaw in two days that was within her budget. She booked a hotel for a night in Liverpool. For the price it had surprisingly good rates and reviews.

She flipped to the next page in the journal.

When I arrived in Dublin today, I couldn't believe how amazing it was. I walked through the parks and enjoyed the architecture of the city. It was late in the day so when I came across a hostel I booked a bed for the night. I met a girl named Julie, she is from the UK. We played cards for a couple hours. She has to go back to Liverpool tomorrow. She plans on taking the ferry in the morning. She invited me to go along and said I could crash on her couch for a few days if I'd like. She seems like a really nice girl. I'm in the bed right next to hers. I feel like it's probably fate that we met so I'm going to go with her tomorrow.

Famous flipped to the next page hoping she could find out more about this Julie.

Julie and I almost missed the ferry today but we made it just in time. I'm sitting on the ferry now, the water is rough, it's raining like mad, and it's extremely cold outside. I'm excited to see Liverpool more about that later.

Famous decided she could read more tomorrow and turned on the TV. She thought about reading a letter from her mom but got interested in a detective show and soon fell asleep.

CHAPTER TWENTY NINE

ARE YOU FOLLOWING ME?

When Famous woke up she realized she had slept later than she wanted. She had to hurry if she was going to make the ferry in time. She brushed her hair, brushed her teeth, grabbed her stuff and ran out the door. She made it to the subway and got to the ferry just in time before they were pulling the gang planks. She was grateful that food and drinks were included in the ticket on the ferry. She desperately wanted some coffee and breakfast. After they pushed off she found her way to the restaurant. She lucked out and got the last open table.

A lovely woman about the same age as Famous walked up to her table, "hi my name is Juliet, I was wondering if you'd mind if I joined you."

"Absolutely, it would be nice to have the company. My name is Famous, it's nice to meet you Juliet."

"Wow, I'm sure you hear it all the time, but what an unusual name. Will this be your first time to Liverpool?"

"Yes it is, how about you?"

"No, I go back and forth all the time for work." A server walked up and took their order, they were both happy when she reappeared with their coffee. "It seems like I never get up in time to have coffee before I have to leave for the ferry. Every single time I try, but you know how it is, it just never works out. I hit the sleep timer for just five more minutes."

"I overslept and didn't even get a chance to take a shower. I've booked a hotel for the night and fly out of Liverpool tomorrow."

"Oh, where are you going?"

"Warsaw, Poland."

"What's in Warsaw?"

"I'm really not sure yet, it's kind of hard to explain and a very long story."

"I've got time, that is, if you want to tell me." Famous tried to give her the short version of why she was going to Warsaw. "That's some story, I'm sorry about your mother."

"Thanks," Famous thought about the several times she had told this story and was trying to remember if Juliet was the first person to say that. So much had happened that she just couldn't remember. "She was amazing and I miss her very much."

"Well I think it's awesome that you are doing this and I bet she would be really proud of you." The server brought their breakfast and set it on the table in front of them. She came back a few moments later to refill their coffee. They sat quietly and ate their breakfast. After breakfast they hung out together and walked around the ferry. It had started raining and the wind picked up so they stayed inside.

They talked the whole time they were on the ferry. Shared stories of travel, their work, and just life in general. Time went by very quickly, Famous never got back to reading her mom's journal. She thought about it at one point but didn't want to be rude. She knew she would have time at the hotel. She found Juliet to be delightful to chat with. Before they docked in Liverpool they exchanged emails.

"It's too bad you've already booked a room, you could have stayed at my place."

"Well thanks anyways, that's super nice of you."

"I wish I didn't have to work today, I'd give you a tour." The boat docked, Famous had to go through UK customs so they said goodbye and went their separate ways. After she cleared customs she was surprised to see Juliet waiting for her. "I thought maybe you could use a ride.

I'm going right past the World Museum, if you want a lift."

"Yes, I'd love that, I guess it's just my lucky day." She walked with her out to her car. It was a short ride to the museum.

"You're going to love the museum and because it's in the city center you can catch a train anywhere. I hope you enjoy your visit. One day doesn't seem like enough time in Liverpool to me."

"Yeah I guess I should have stayed a few days, but I managed to get a cheap flight." Juliet pulled in front of the museum and came to a stop. "I guess this is where I get off, it was a true pleasure meeting you. Let's keep in touch."

"Absolutely, you've got my email, I can't wait to hear the rest of your story. Good luck Famous."

Famous closed the car door and waved one last goodbye before heading into the museum. It was a grand building, there was so much to see, a planetarium, an aquarium, dinosaurs, and the list went on. She knew she would never be able to see everything. Walking through the museum, she had a feeling like someone was following her. She kept glancing back, but no one was there. At one point, she saw a reflection in the glass, but when she turned around, nothing. Now she was beginning to think she was just paranoid.

She was so distracted, it was becoming obvious that she couldn't enjoy the museum. She started to make her way to the exit when a man approached her. "Famous?"

She was staring at him, but had no clue who he could be. "Do I know you?"

"Yes and no, I met you as a small child. You were with your mother."

"Listen, I know I don't even resemble my mother. You can't possibly tell me you recognize me from when I was a baby. Have you been following me?"

"I followed you from Ireland."

"I should call the police."

"I didn't mean to startle or ambush you. I wanted to talk to you on the ferry, but you were with that girl the whole time. I was a friend of your mother's, I called Ellie to get a room and she told me you were there. I couldn't get there until last night. She told me you were taking the ferry to Liverpool.

My name is Johnathon, I'm certain I must be in your mother's journal. I've been investigating that castle for years. Just when I had nearly given up, Ellie called and told me what happened to you. You must come back

213

with me." He had his hand on her arm, she pulled away.

"Are you crazy? I'm not going to go backwards. I'm on a specific path my mom wanted me to follow."

"Dar would want you to do this."

"I'm not turning around. I have a hotel here in Liverpool and a flight to Warsaw. I fully plan on making that flight. Plus it sounded like my mom tried to go back a couple of times."

He had a briefcase in his hands, "If I could just show you."

"I'm terribly sorry... Um..."

"Johnathon"

"Johnathon, again really sorry, but I have to do this. Now if you'll excuse me, I think I'll be going." She started to walk away, "You know, I can meet you after I finish this journey on my way back to the States. I don't think it will do any good, but I did plan on visiting with Ellie and Edmund anyway."

"Will you at least hear me out?"

She shrugged, "I guess, but it won't change anything."

Johnathon smiled, "Let me take you to dinner, okay?"

"Okay, I guess if you really want to. Can meet me at my hotel?"

"Sure, I wonder if they have any more rooms available." He looked excited and Famous figured it would be easier to let him down if she heard him out.

"You can check," she told him the name of the hotel. "I found them online. I was surprised at how reasonable their rates are."

"You know that place is haunted, right?" Famous gave him a look like she didn't believe him. "Seriously look it up, it's on my list of places to stay. I just hadn't made it to Liverpool. How exciting, I have a rental car coming to pick me up soon, I can give you a lift."

"Well now that I am not so freaked out about being followed, I'd like to look around here for another hour or so."

"No problem, I will meet you out front at your leisure. I still have to run with the rental guy and fill out paperwork." She agreed and turned back toward the exhibit area. She had another thought, but when she looked back, he was gone. Famous made her way through a few exhibits, after an hour had gone by she headed for the exit. When she went out the door Johnathon was there waiting.

CHAPTER THIRTY

FATE

Liverpool looked like it would be an interesting city. She suddenly wished she was staying a few days. The weather wasn't her favorite, raining and cold. She still enjoyed watching out the window at the buildings on the way to the hotel. "So the hotel is haunted, huh?"

"Yes, it's considered to be one of the most haunted in Liverpool." The hotel was conveniently located near a train station. Famous was impressed by the grand size and appearance as they approached the front of the hotel. She was surprised by all of the services and amenities offered as she checked in. She thought about asking about the hauntings, but figured she'd just do a search on her phone.

Johnathon was elated when he was able to get a room. His room was on the same floor as hers. Famous went to her room after telling Johnathon he could come get her for dinner around seven. The room was tastefully decorated. She walked in to check out the bathroom when she came back there was a girl digging in her purse. "Excuse me?" The girl disappeared into thin air. Famous was taken aback, and demised it and that she was just seeing things. She was sure that Johnathon had put the ghostly thoughts in her head.

She sat down on the bed and took out her mother's journal, along with the pack of letters. She made a few notes in her own journal about the day so far. She flipped open her mother's journal.

When Julie and I reached the port she took me sightseeing. We went to the World Museum, and several other historical markers. Liverpool offered so many options for sightseeing. Julie was a great tour guide, I am so lucky to have met her. She took me all over the city. Last night I told her about Angelica, the castle, and the curse. I told her about all of the stuff that Johnathon had showed me. She works for some kind of historical association so she plans to do some checking on it. Angelica's story really makes me sad for her, but I have to find my girl.

Famous heard a knock on the door, but when she opened the door there was no one there. She thought she saw a bellboy down the hall but at second glance the hall was empty. Her thoughts went back to Angelica and her mother. She wished her mother had been clear about the historical association that Julie had worked for. She looked at the time and realized she better get in the shower if she were going to be presentable for dinner. So she would have to pick up where she left off later.

She was running late, Johnathon had come to get her before she was ready. She invited him in and apologized for her tardiness. They decided to eat at the restaurant in the hotel. They talked about the history of the hotel and the supernatural guests that supposedly live there on the way down. One he had mentioned bared resemblance to the girl she thought she had seen digging in her purse. She told Johnathon about the experience and that she had just dismissed it.

"There is something about you and your mom that seems to draw the supernatural to you."

"My mom always said she had a connection to the psychic world. I can say she definitely had some premonitions. Maybe she was psychic, she always seemed to know things before they happened."

"I believe that, I wish I had had more time with her."

"Yeah me too." Famous sounded saddened at the thought of her being gone.

After ordering, Johnathon opened a file of paperwork and pictures. She recognized the castle in many of the pictures. One had a big blurry spot inside the door. There were a few with blurry spots in the kitchen. "These are weird," she glanced up at Johnathon.

"Those are the ones she was in. I was severely disappointed when I developed them and they were blurry. Your mom made a connection with her. I tried, but I refused her tea saying I didn't like tea. She studied me before saying anything and I took her picture. I'll admit I should have asked, she got angry. I didn't know what happened, but the next thing I knew my camera was in her hand and being thrown out the door. I ran out after it and the big door slammed shut."

"So did your camera break?"

"Yeah, but thankfully I was still able to recover the SD card. I often wonder if I had just drank the tea what would have happened. I met your mom not too long after that. After I heard her story I begged her to go there with me. Apparently she did go back at some point, but I wasn't with her. I was hoping you could go there with me." He showed her a few old fairytales he had run across. Then he showed her some documentation on the history of ownership dating back over one hundred years.

"I still haven't found anything concrete in historical data. I know it sounds stupid, but of all the places I have investigated this one haunts me."

"Why is that?"

"Probably because it's the one that alluded me. I stopped and started this investigation so many times. I had to earn a living so I'd put it on the back burner. I even did some work as a substitute professor in several universities. One in particular led me back to this castle." About that time their dinner arrived.

"I'm sure that Ellie told you that I'm on a specific journey. I would love to help you out, but it's not a good time for me right now." She nibbled on her salad in silence. In her mind there was really nothing more to say. Jonathon wanted to tell her about the book, but it wasn't the time. She wasn't open to hearing about it.

"Well I am meeting the realtor there in a few days. I will actually be able to go inside and finally get to tour the full grounds inside and out."

"Why haven't you done that before?"

"Don't think I haven't tried, this is the first time I have been able to get in touch with them. I think it's a new realtor and the others before would go in one time and never again. I have been put off dozens of times. They rescheduled again and again and then finally would give me a number to a different realtor.

I have gotten the run around more times than you could imagine. That's why I wanted you to go, it's a first. I couldn't believe it when I called Ellie to reserve a room and she told me you were there. She told me what had happened to you. I immediately thought that it was fate. Famous, I really believe that this is fate."

"Did you talk to my mom after she left?"

"A few times, but she was so focused on you. She was so completely happy being your mom." Johnathon was staring at Famous, what he said had made her smile. "Is there anything I can say that will change your mind? I will even pay for your travel, including your ticket to Warsaw from Dublin."

"I don't think so, I'm truly sorry."

"Famous, just tell me you'll sleep on it. Here," he handed her a business card. "Email or call me tomorrow. Maybe we can meet for breakfast."

"I'll be leaving early." Famous asked the server for her bill. "I really am sorry, Johnathon, but what I am doing is so important to me. I feel like I have to continue on, I just…" She shook her head like there were no words she could use that would express her feelings.

Johnathon could tell she was struggling with her decision. He wanted to keep talking, but at the same time he didn't want to push her. He was thinking there was a chance albeit, a small chance, it was still a chance. "Just think it over, okay." The server came with the bill but Johnathon grabbed it before Famous could. "Please, let me get this, I really appreciate you talking with me."

"That's really not necessary."

He handed the server his credit card, "No really I want to."

"Thank you, it was a nice meal. I should be heading up to bed, I have an early morning. Are you going up?"

"I think I might hang out and ask some of the employees some questions. I talked to the manager and he said it was fine. I figure I may as well since I am here."

"That's cool, have a good night. Oh and good luck with… everything."

"Thanks, and again, I hope you'll at least think about it. This is the opportunity I have been waiting for."

She smiled and headed for the exit. Famous went up to her room and laid down on the bed. She set the alarm on her phone and turned on the TV. She was thinking that it was a little challenging to understand because their accent was so thick. She thought about reading more in the journal or one of her mom's letters, but her eyes were so tired. She drifted off to sleep.

The alarm woke her, it felt like she had only slept minutes not hours. She got up, showered, and got dressed. It only took a few minutes for her to pack the few things she had taken out of her bag the night before. She had arranged a shuttle to the airport. It was raining so hard she nearly got soaked going from the hotel doors to the shuttle. Famous got to the airport two hours before her flight. After she got through security she went to get coffee and breakfast. There were several options for a breakfast sandwich.

She pulled out the pack of letters from her mom. She opened the next letter to read while she was eating. The picture inside was of them on a vacation in Mexico with big funny sombrero's holding maracas. She had to laugh at how silly they looked.

Famous,
I know you are probably only reading a letter every couple of days and that is great. I hope it's because you are so busy with life. Remember, this is a journey of healing and self-discovery so don't hold onto the past too

tightly. I'm so proud of you, I hope you always remember that. I hope your journey is as special to you as mine was to me. I'm sure you are starting to individualize it more and more because it is about you. I hope it will lead you from my path to yours. Anyway enough of that mushy stuff.

This trip was amazing, snorkeling, swimming with dolphins, the walks on the beach, and most of all laughing together. I hope this is one of your fondest memories, because it sure was mine. Thank you so much for this. I am so grateful I was up to it.

I keep wondering where you are as your reading this. I can only tell you where I am and hope it brings back a great memory. I am watching you swim in the pool on our last night of vacation. I planned to have that talk with you, but we were having so much fun I couldn't ruin it. Oh well, tomorrow's another day. It's hard when I've been feeling so much better. Well it looks like you're getting out of the pool so I better go.

Much love,
Mom

Famous was smiling, it was a fond memory. She folded the letter and put it away. After she finished a second cup she went to her gate. She was thinking it would be close to time to start boarding. When she reached the gate she saw that the plane was delayed. There wasn't a time posted and when she inquired, they didn't have any answers for her. There was a crazy lightning storm so the planes were grounded.

Famous took out her mom's journal to pick up where she left off, but a crack of lightning hit the ground just outside the window. She was mesmerized by the lightning for a few minutes. She finally opened the journal,

What a great day with Julie, we even stopped by her work today. She works closely with historical associations all over the world. She was able to locate some information on the castle today. I don't think the information went back far enough, but I had her forward it to Johnathon. I was thinking that if I had the time I would check into this whole curse business. Julie and I talked about how disturbing it would be to spend all of your existence trapped, eternity can be a very long time.

A little old woman sat next to Famous, she smiled and said good morning.

"Good morning, looks like we may be delayed for a while."

"Yes I think so, it's a good time to read a book." She pointed to the journal in Famous' hand.

"Oh this, well it's my mother's journal, she passed away a few years ago and…" her voice trailed off. Famous was thinking that it was a little odd that she would begin a conversation with a complete stranger that way.

"You must miss her very much. It's hard to lose someone you love. You sound like you're from America, are you vacationing?" Famous felt compelled to tell her the story and she sat with her for what seemed like hours telling her about the journey she had been on. When she got to the part about the witch the little old woman stopped her and interupted. "She is still in the castle after all of these years?"

"Yes and the longer I sit here the more I realize it's a mistake for me to get on this plane. There must be something I can do. I remember back in the library where I worked I read several books on curses and breaking spells. It just may be possible, maybe that is my path. Hey um, I'm sorry I don't know your name, but I have to go."

"Wait child that could be very dangerous, especially if you don't know what you're doing. You must seek guidance, give me your hand child." She looked at Famous' palm, closed her eyes, said some strange words, and placed an amulet on her palm. Famous had seen this amulet before, but where? She closed her eyes, where had she seen it. Then it came to her, it had been in the stuff with her mother's journals. And it was in her back pack.

CHAPTER THIRTY ONE

THE RIGHT PATH

When she opened her eyes the woman was gone. Famous looked all around for the old woman, but she was nowhere in sight. She shoved the amulet in her pocket. She placed her mother's journal back in her bag. She could see that the lightning and the rain had gotten much worse. She began to walk quickly toward the front of the Airport. This was her path to follow and she knew it.

She kept hearing the old woman's voice say 'seek guidance.' Where was she going to find guidance? Johnathon, could he be the one for which she was to seek guidance? Her phone wasn't working in Liverpool. Maybe she could get on Wi-Fi somewhere and email him. It was only a fifteen minute taxi ride back to the hotel. She went straight to the front desk "Hello, can you tell me if my friend Johnathan Dowel has checked out?"

"Yes ma'am, he has, you wouldn't by chance be Famous would you?"

"Yes I am, why?"

"He left something for you, but I must see your identification." Famous dug out her passport and handed it to the woman. "Well, Famous, quite a name you've got, I'll just get that for you."

"Thank you." Famous stood there fidgeting and looking at the time. She couldn't remember the ferry times. The woman came out of the office and handed Famous an envelope. The woman turned to go back in the office. "Excuse me, would you by chance know the ferry schedule for today?"

"I'm sorry I don't, but you could look it up online."

"Thank you," Famous put the envelope in her bag and left the hotel. She took a taxi to the ferry port. She got to the ticket office, but it was closed for lunch. She waited the ten minutes for it to reopen. "Hello, I'd like to get the next ferry to Dublin please."

"Let me take a look, okay we do have some space. I just need your passport please. Famous dug through her backpack and realized the woman at the hotel hadn't given it back. She explained what had happened to the woman. She asked if she could just pay for her ticket now and pick it up when she returned. "Well, I suppose that would be no different than you purchasing it online."

"Thank you, thank you so much."

"You better get going you haven't much time."

Famous ran out into the parking area, she looked around, but there was no taxi in sight. She ran back in, "Can you call me a taxi, it's really urgent that I get back to Dublin." The woman nodded, called, and said it would only be a few minutes. Famous paced until the taxi arrived.

She jumped in and handed the driver the address, "As quickly as you can and then can you wait for me. I left my passport at the front desk. I will pay for the meter while you wait. They are a little slow, but please wait. I really don't want to miss the ferry."

"No problem, ma'am."

She was grateful for her rain slicker, it had become a torrential downpour. The driver weaved through traffic and it didn't take long before she was sloshing through a puddle and into the hotel. There was no one at the front desk. She rang the bell, no one came. She rang the bell several more times. Finally she saw a bellboy, "excuse me," he didn't look at her. "Excuse me," she heard the office door open. The same woman appeared, "I tried to get the bellboy's attention, but…" Famous glanced and it was as if he had disappeared.

"What bellboy?" Famous thought back to the ghosts, but she didn't have time for this now.

"I need my passport, you didn't give it back."

"I'm sure I did, ma'am. I must have, as you can see it's not here."

Famous stared at her for a minute, "You took it with you when you went into that door right there. I am in a tremendous hurry, please go get my passport."

The woman turned, "I'll go take a look." She was gone for what seemed like an eternity. "You were right, I am so sorry ma'am." She handed her the passport, "I truly am sorry for the inconvenience." Famous practically ripped it from her hand and ran out the door. She sloshed back through the puddle and got into the taxi.

"Okay, back to the ferry please." She hadn't realized the driver wasn't in the car. She glanced around the car. "You have got to be kidding!" She looked all around, but it was raining so hard. She couldn't see him anywhere. She opened the door to look for another taxi or a shuttle... something, anything. A few minutes had gone by. She was soaked, the driver finally came out carrying a coffee. "I told you I was in a hurry."

"Don't worry, I'll get you there in time." She climbed back in, slammed the door, and buckled up. "Easy there," he could see she was annoyed. He sped away from the hotel. He drove much faster than he had on the way to the hotel. Famous was tilting from side to side as he sped through the traffic. They reached the ferry just as they were getting ready to pull the gangplank.

"Wait, please wait, I have to pick up my ticket from the office." Famous' screamed at the man.

He waved back at her, "I will give you two minutes, but no more." The man looked at his watch as Famous' ran to the ticket office.

"I almost didn't think you're going to make it." The woman looked at Famous' passport and handed her the ticket.

"Thank you so much," Famous snatched the ticket from her hand. She ran back to the ferry, showed the man her ticket, and he motioned her to board.

"You sure are lucky, you made it just in time." Famous boarded the ferry, shook the rain off her coat, and went to find a cup of coffee. Famous was so cold and wet, she was shivering. The server brought her a cup of coffee and a towel to dry off with.

"Thanks I'm freezing, this will really help." She took out the envelope from Jonathan and pulled out the letter inside. The letter had gotten wet and the words were blurry.

Famous

I am so grateful that you changed your mind. …get to Dublin … the archive library… Seven amulet's…witch's curse

She held the paper up and tried to make out the words. The first sentence was the only somewhat complete sentence that she could read. She had felt something else in the envelope. When she pulled it out it was at another amulet. She pulled the one from her pocket and they were nearly identical. There were a few markings or pictures on each one that made them different. Famous was thinking she would call Jonathan when she got to Dublin. Her sim card worked fine in Dublin.

She took out her journal, ripped out a page and tried to make out some of the words on Jonathan's letter. It was no use, she could not make heads or tails of what he had said. The server came, refilled her coffee, and brought her a menu. "You should try the soup, it's great on a cold day like this."

"Maybe I will, let me take a look." Famous looked at the menu, but her mind was elsewhere. The server had come back twice before Famous ordered a grilled cheese sandwich with a tomato bisque soup. She had finally warmed up when she was reminded that she didn't put her mother's journal back in the zip lock. She dug it out, luckily she had shoved it down farther when she put in Jonathon's letter. It had gotten wet, but it was still legible, for the most part. She opened it to the page she was reading in the airport.

I know that the history will help, but I told Julie to contact someone that was involved in Wicca, also known as witchcraft, maybe they would know something. I leave tomorrow morning for Warsaw and I know I am only days away. Perhaps when I get back, I can help Angelica. A few days more.

A small note was attached.
Famous
Wow, there is so much to say here, but I shall not say any of it. I will only say there was an amulet in the box with my journals. It is for you and the rest of your journey. There are seven of them, you will need them all. I wish you the best of luck. The following pages will become clear to you when the time is right.
Much love, be safe my darling,
Mom

Famous didn't understand, she flipped to the next page. The page was blurry, and the page after and the page after. None of it made sense. What did she mean? Famous put everything back in her backpack when her soup arrived. Her mind raced, seven amulets, she only had three. She hoped she had three, she looked in the other Ziploc with what she thought was miscellaneous souvenirs and pulled out the third. She was grateful she had brought the trinkets. It too was nearly identical, she stuffed it in her pocket with the others. After eating lunch she must have looked at her watch a dozen times over the duration of the trip back to Dublin.

She had so many questions. Where were the other amulets? How would she find them all in time? What was she to do with them? She paced back and forth on the ferry looking out to see if they were getting closer to land. The clocked seemed to be standing still. Famous was the first to get off the ferry.

She kept walking and looking at her phone searching for enough bars to make a call. It took her a while to dig out Jonathon's card. She dialed his number and waited for it to ring. It went straight to voicemail, 'Jonathan you must call me immediately I'm in Dublin. Your letter got wet and I couldn't read it. I don't know where I am supposed to go.' Famous hung up the phone and went back to the archive library. That was one of the few words she could read.

The same woman was at the information desk that had helped her the previous day. "Hello again, I have a rather strange question. I was in here the other day looking for some history on a castle, do you remember me?"

"Yes of course I do, it would be hard to forget someone named Famous. I thought you were going to Liverpool. What can I do for you?"

"I did, but realized that wasn't the path I needed to take. Anyway, apparently, I didn't ask you the right question. I am wondering if you have a book that talks about seven amulets and the witch's curse."

"That isn't a strange question at all. We did have such a book for years and years, but recently it's gone missing."

Famous stood there silently for several minutes. "Missing, I'm not quite sure I understand, are you saying it was checked out and they lost it?"

"No, more like it was stolen, actually it was like in the vanished into thin air. We're sure it was a one of a kind too, a handwritten book, we had in a glass case. It was there one day and gone the next. There is absolutely no explanation for it, the glass case was intact and locked. How would an American know of such a book?"

"It's a long story. I really needed to see that book, I just don't know what I'll do now."

The woman wrote down a phone number. "I'm not sure if this will help but a few months ago there was a student at the university studying witchcraft, curses, and medieval times. I don't know for sure but he may have gotten permission to copy the book. He said he needed it for his class."

"Thanks so much, it's worth a try."

Famous stepped outside to make the call. His name was Daniel, the phone rang and rang with no answer. Not even a voicemail, "So what now?" She tried to think of her options, should she go back to Ellie's? Should she wait for Jonathon or Daniels call? Daniel probably wouldn't call because she couldn't leave a voicemail. What to do, those words ran through her mind over and over. She knew she would figure it out, there had to be an answer and she was going to find it.

CHAPTER THIRTY TWO

SO WHAT NOW?

When her phone rang it startled her. "Hello"

"Hi, I just missed a call from this number."

"Daniel?"

"Yes this is Daniel, who am I speaking with?"

"My name is Famous, I understand you may have copied the book about the seven amulets and the witch's curse." There was a silence on the phone for several seconds. "Hello, Daniel are you there?"

"I'm here, I'm sorry I don't think I can help you."

"You don't even know why I'm calling."

"Yes I do, you just told me and I can't help you. I really have to go."

"Please don't hang up on me, I really need your help." It was too late he had already hung up. Famous dialed his number again and it rang and rang. She tried several more times until he finally answered.

"Listen I said I can't help you, stop calling me."

"I only need your copy and you'll never hear from me again."

There was a silence again on the phone. He spoke in a whisper, "That book caused so many problems in my life. I try to get rid of my copy several times only to have it reappear. Even if I try to give it to you, it would do you no good."

"Can you meet me somewhere?" He was hesitant but finally agreed to come to the library. Famous walked back inside and wandered through the aisles of books. She found herself in the supernatural section. She saw several titles on the witch's, ferries, and druids. It was a rather large selection. She took a book of spells, sat down at the table, and began to read.

"Are you Famous?" she nodded. He placed a stack of papers on the table in front of her. "Well here it is, the minute I leave it'll disappear. Then I will find it somewhere in my possessions. It's a very difficult book to read, written in old times, with a very old English and Gaelic. Why'd you need it?"

"It's a really long story. The short version is I have three of the seven amulets. When I get the rest, I will need this, to break a curse."

"Are you nuts? You should never try to mess with a witch's curse." The librarian shushed them. He started to whisper, "I don't want any part of this. You have no idea what I've been through."

"I don't remember asking you for your help. I only wanted a copy of the book."

"Fine, there you go." He started to walk away and then turned back. "I wonder if I help you, if it will help me." Famous shrugged her shoulders. "If there is even a small chance, I'm in. I want to be rid of that book once and for all. I even tried to burn it."

"I don't understand why it bothers you so much that it keeps coming back."

"I can't explain it, but I've been cursed since I have had it. So where do we go from here?"

"I'm not sure we go anywhere from here, I am going to read it and see where it takes me. Did you read it?"

"It is very hard to read, my college professor read it and gave me the gist of it." The librarian shushed them again. "We should get out of here." She put the book back that she had been reading. Then picked up the stack of papers and followed him out of the library. "So, basically, there are seven amulets, hold on, I have to think. Give me those papers. "He snatched them out of her hands and flipped through the pages. "Here it is," he pointed to the page.

This child must possess the seven amulets,
Past
Present
Eternity
Love
Purity
Safety
Forgiveness

She looks at Daniel, "The child, what child?"

"I don't know, this is one of the few pages that I even understand."

"So now, I need to find several more amulets and a child. That's just perfect."

Her phone rang, it was Jonathon. "Famous, I got your message, are you still in Dublin?"

"Yes."

"Did you get the book?"

"Well kind of," she explained the whole situation to him. Daniel was standing there listening to the conversation. He seemed back and forth about whether or not he really wanted to get involved in whatever this was. She glanced up at him and smiled. Famous thought that there was something in him that said, help her. There was also probably a loud voice in his head screaming, run!

She hung up the phone and said she needed to go. "Wait, what about me?"

"It doesn't involve you and you look like you don't want it to."

"Oh," he held the papers up, "Really? Then I'll just be going now," he started to walk to his car.

She followed him, "I'm going to need those papers."

"Not without me." He opened his car door and climbed in. He unlocked the passenger door and motioned for her to get in. She climbed in and he looked over at her. "Where to?"

"You don't want to know."

Famous gave him directions from her phone. They drove for a while outside of Dublin. It had turned to night and the rain had finally stopped. They didn't talk much at first then he started asking questions. This led to Famous giving him the full rundown. When she asked him to stop, there was nothing there. She slid on her rubber boots and got out of the car. She dug out her pocket knife and flashlight. He followed her into a large field. The ground was wet and muddy. She looked back at Daniel's feet, "You might want to wait here."

She walked until she came to a large tree. Daniel could barely see her, just a small light in the field. She heard the wind whisper and swore it said for her to leave now. Of course it was her imagination, it had to be, didn't it? Her mind wandered back to the monster story. She imagined her mother saying, monsters don't live in trees Famous. She shined her light on the tree and looked at the coordinates Jonathon had sent to her phone. "This is it," she yelled to Daniel.

She walked around the tree shining the light on the base of the tree. Finally she came to a big knot on the root, she stood in front of it with her back to the tree and shined her flashlight. There it was, a grave stone, Famous kept thinking, this is just creepy. I've now become a grave robber. She walked up to the stone and dug the amulet out of the back with her knife.

She heard something, it sounded like it was running at her. She shoved the amulet in her pocket and ran. Famous looked back but it was so dark. There was definitely something following, no chasing, her. Daniel saw her running toward him, she fell face first in the mud. She jumped back up. Daniel opened the door, she jumped in, and slammed it shut. "Go!"

He stepped on the gas and sped away. They were a mile or so down the road when he looked at Famous. He could not contain his laughter. She was head to toe mud. He reached in his glovebox where he had one of those micro fiber cloths. "So let me guess, there was one of the amulets there?"

"Lucky number four," She checked her phone for another message from Jonathon. "One more to go."

"One, but there's seven. What about the other two?"

"They are there waiting for us. Unfortunately I don't know where the last one is. I do know where we are going to end up though so we'll just head west." They drove until they were nearly at the coast.

He pulled into a pub, "I have to get something to eat." They went in, he ordered some fish and chips. She ordered the same. Famous told Daniel about her mother's journal being blurry. She took it out of the bag and showed him. She opened to the page and she could read part of the first sentence.

I went back to the

"This is new!"

"What?"

"I swear I couldn't read any of this page earlier." She turned back a page and read the note to Daniel. "Oh, Daniel, I get it, I totally get it now."

"Great, do you want to explain it to me?"

"She said the following pages will become clear to you when the time is right. It was a little cryptic, well not really, she spelled it out. Now I get it, I will eventually be able to read it." She looked at the page and another word had appeared. "Castle, she went back to the castle. She didn't go to Warsaw. You see, the first time you looked at it the word castle was definitely not clear."

"This has to be the craziest thing I have ever seen in my life. If I hadn't seen it with my own two eyes, I wouldn't believe it. Actually, I'm still not sure I do believe it. It's like that ridiculous book. I can't explain what has happened since I copied it." The server brought their dinner, "Thanks, this looks great." She smiled and asked if there was anything else she could bring. "No, thank you."

They ate in silence for a while. Famous' phone chimed. She looked and it was another message from Jonathon. It said, we are having a hard time deciphering the clue to the last one. You two should come to Ellie's and get some rest.

"So, Daniel, want to stay in a castle tonight?" She showed him the message.

He shrugged, "I guess I don't have any other plans now." Famous texted him back that they would be there in an hour or two. "Famous, I'm confused about a few things."

"A few things, really? Because I'm confused about a lot of things. I think things will be clearer when we get to Ellie and Edmond's. At least I hope so." They finished the rest of their dinner and got back on the road. Famous set the GPS on her phone.

The drive went by quickly for Famous. Daniel talked about all of the unfortunate incidences that happened since he had read the book. It wasn't just him either. He said his professor had experienced a series of bad luck incidents as well. "He was only a sub for a semester, so I haven't seen him since."

Famous had Daniel slow down as they passed the witch's castle. He nearly stopped and they both stared, they saw nothing but a dark old castle. He pulled into the drive at Ellie and Edmond's. Jonathon came out to greet them. Daniel recognized him right away, "Professor Dowel?" Famous looked confused for a minute before it all came into place for her.

Famous smiled at Johnathon, "Good evening, Jonathon, I'm still a little confused. But I think it's starting to come together for me. I just don't understand if you had all of this information at your fingertips, why am I here?" Ellie came out and called everyone in. Daniel followed Famous inside. Famous hugged Ellie, "Why didn't you tell me?"

She smiled, "You had to follow your path. You had things to experience, people to meet," she glanced at Daniel. "You had to be compelled to make your own decisions."

"Jonathon, I still don't understand." Ellie ushered everyone into the beanbag room. They all sat by the fire.

"I wished I could tell you everything, Famous, but I can't. Things will be clear when the time is right." Famous' head was reeling. She was trying to put everything in place. Daniel sat quietly and listened as Jonathon explained that Famous would learn all she needed to know from her mother. "Everything is as it's supposed to be."

Jonathon looked over at Daniel, "Daniel when you brought that book to me, I couldn't believe it. It supposedly was a fairy tale, telling about the princess Angelica. What a stroke of luck that I subbed for your class. I just couldn't figure out why, when you gave me your copy it disappeared. Fortunately, I had written down all of the clues to the amulets." He explained that he had gone to see the book at the library and it was gone. "The librarian had given me your number. So I hoped she would do the same if Famous went there."

They sat quietly for a few minutes, Famous spoke first, "So what now?"

"We have to find the last amulet, but for tonight, I say, we get some sleep. We have only a few days until I meet the realtor."

"Famous, you'll be in the sunshine room again and Daniel you'll be bunking in the same room as Jonathon so, he'll show you to your room. We have a full house so I have an early morning with breakfast. I'm turning in for the night."

"Okay, goodnight Ellie."

CHAPTER THIRTY THREE

THINGS BECOME CLEAR

Famous said good night, took her bag, and climbed the stairs to her room. She laid back on the bed. She opened her journal and wrote down everything that had happened. Then she followed up on another page with all her thoughts. She drifted off to sleep with her journal on her chest. She was dreaming of her mother. She was there at the castle holding Famous. Angelica was there, she was beautiful just as her mother described. They were talking, but Famous was too young to understand.

Something startled her awake. She sat up in the bed. One of the amulets had fallen from her pocket and was laying on the floor. She picked it up and placed it back in her pocket. She felt compelled to grab her mother's journal and open it.

I went back to the castle today. I had to talk to Angelica to see if there was a way to break the curse. I went to the door, but she wouldn't come to the door. I sat in front of the door for hours. I thought I would fall asleep, I was so tired. I was about to give up when the door creaked open. I went inside and she gave me a cup of tea. It was the same as before, it took a while for everything to become clear. I asked her about breaking the curse. She told me that there was a way it could be broken. I asked her to tell me how.

She said:

You must hike to the ice caves deep in the snow.
Go to the Monk, he is the one who will Know.
A child, the child that waits for you, holds the key.
A key, the key, to setting me free.
Again I woke up on the steps in front of the door.

Famous turned the page, but it was blurry. She was the one who held the key, how is that possible? Famous laid down, she just couldn't sleep. She read the words again and again. She turned the page, but it was still blurry. She finally dozed off, but her sleep was restless. She tossed and turned.

It was early when Famous stepped into the shower and let the water run over her head. She was exhausted, it had been a long night. Actually the whole day yesterday, not just the night. Her mind kept going back to her holding the key. It didn't make sense, how could a baby hold a key to a curse that was hundreds of years old.

She toweled off, brushed her teeth, and got dressed. Ellie was in the kitchen when she came down the stairs. "Coffee, Famous?"

"Of course."

Ellie poured her a cup, "How did you sleep?"

"Not well, actually, strange dreams, and I tossed and turned all night. How about you?"

"About the same, I guess in some small way, I always knew this day would come. Now that it's here, well I am a little nervous about the outcome."

"I don't understand."

"You will, soon, Famous, very soon."

Slowly others came into the kitchen seeking their first cup of coffee. They sat around the table talking. Famous got up and helped Ellie cook breakfast. Daniel and Jonathon were the last ones to come into the kitchen. Edmond introduced the new guests to her and Daniel, then poured himself a cup of coffee and joined them at the table.

Famous was stirring the beans and frying potatoes. There was bacon and sausage keeping warm in the oven. Ellie was scrambling eggs and buttering toast. Famous looked at the table, it was nearly full. There were fifteen if you counted her and Ellie. She wondered how

Ellie did it. So many people to prepare meals for.

"Famous, you're being awfully quiet, what are you thinking?" She looked back at Daniel, he had walked up behind her. She hadn't even noticed, she shrugged and shook her head, as if to say nothing much. He whispered in her ear, "Anything new in the journal?"

"Yes, actually, a lot new. I'll show you after breakfast, you won't believe it. I didn't look this morning, there could be more now for all I know. You want to help me set the table?"

"Sure." Famous showed him where everything was. They placed the dishes on the table, Ellie started setting out glasses of juice. Edmond came in and started placing all of the food down the center of the long table. Daniel was thinking how delicious everything looked, he was starved. "Ellie this looks amazing."

"Thanks Daniel, but in all fairness I couldn't have done it without Famous' help."

Famous smiled, "You do all the time, but thank you." She sat down between Daniel and Jonathon. The plates of food rotated around the table. Everyone taking a little of this and a little of that. "Ellie it really is a delightful feast."

After breakfast the guests slowly meandered to their rooms or off to go sightseeing. Famous started to help Ellie clean up the table.

"Famous, you have more important things to do, Edmond and I will get this."

Jonathon stood up, he tapped Daniel on the shoulder, and indicated for him and Famous to follow him. They went to the bean bag room. He handed Famous the other two amulets. "Ellie found these two and the one that was given to you in the airport. Ellie sent the woman to give it to you. She had hoped it would help you to decide to turn around. That woman's family are white witches. We believe they wrote the book. I found the one I gave you, we've been working on it for months.

There is one more, I know it's near here, I just can't figure it out. I can't tell you the part of the story that is your story Famous, it must come from your mother. I made her a promise if this situation ever came up. Honestly, I never thought I'd be faced with having to keep that promise. The only way I can help is with the translation of the book and finding the amulets."

He asked Daniel to get the copy of the book. "I must have missed something or translated something wrong for the last one." Daniel went back to his room to get the book. Famous had sat down on a bean bag, she was so tired. It was difficult to think. She could hear

Jonathon talking, but couldn't focus on his words. "Famous?"

"I'm sorry, I just zoned out a little. I didn't sleep well last night." Daniel walked back in and handed the stack of papers to Jonathon. He sat down and studied them. "So what does it say?"

"The book tells the story of what happened so many years ago. It talks about the princess, the witch, and the curse. The book continues the story after the princess' death. It says upon the death of the spell caster the spell may be broken by one of a pure heart. Then I lose some of the story, it's like it is missing pages or I'm missing the meaning. It talks about a child and describes seven amulets. With the clues for each and at this point, we have found all but one."

Daniel looked over Jonathon's shoulder. "So each amulet has like a treasure map?" "More like an antiquated riddle. The reason I told you to come here is that the seventh is where the prayer of innocence begins. Angelica was innocent and it was the beginning of it all. There are other clues, but they just don't make sense. Hidden in the place of peace where no word is spoken. What is that? For one the past, will leave, but forgiveness will stay until the child returns."

"So it's already there in the castle." Famous looked hopeful.

"No, it can't be, the seven amulets must cross the threshold at the same time. They cannot be taken into the castle separately." The three of them worked on the clues for hours. Famous thought about the town square where she had been publicly accused. Jonathon had already searched there many times and none of the other clues fit.

Famous went upstairs to get her mother's journal. She sat on the bed and opened it to the last page she had read. She slowly turned the page.

After another evening at Ellie and Edmonds I started off to find my little one. I caught a ride to town, then a bus to Dublin. I waited on standby most of the day for a plane to Russia. The flight seemed very long. I managed to sleep for part of it. When I reached Russia, I had to take a bus to a train and then a train through the night.

I left the train station on foot. It was so cold, I hiked for what seemed like hours. The ice caves were beautiful. I walked around with wonder and awe. I was hiking past the mouth of a cave when I slipped. I must have slid for fifty feet before my leg hit a massive chunk of ice. I heard a snap and screamed in pain.

I laid there until the cold crept into my bones. It was at that moment I knew I was going to die if I didn't do something. I crawled and dragged myself back the way I had come. I slid back a few times until I became exhausted. I felt myself slipping away.

I woke up on a makeshift stretcher being dragged through the snow. I was shivering and in so much pain. I passed out again, only the next time I woke I was on a mat of some kind in front of a large fire. I looked around, but there was no one in the room. I tried to sit up, but it was too painful.

The door opened, the monk came into the room. He asked me if I was hungry and gave me some tea. He helped me to sit up and leaned me against a chair. I sipped my tea without saying a word. He brought me soup. I was so hungry, I ate every last drop.

There was a knock on the door. It was Daniel, he wanted to know what was in the journal. Famous caught him up to where she was and continued to read out loud.

The monks were kind to me, they put a splint on my leg and assured me they could get me to a hospital in the coming days. I told the monk who had saved me the story of my journey to find my baby, the witch, and Angelica. He smiled and asked my name. After I told him, he said he had been waiting for me.

Famous turned the page, but again it was blurry. Daniel looked at her, "Why do you suppose you only get a portion of the story at a time?"

Famous shrugged, "Maybe every time I move forward I get another piece of the puzzle. So I can continue to move forward. That's it, that's it, holy cow." She grabbed Daniels hand, "Come on." They ran down the stairs. Famous was yelling for Jonathon. He came out of the kitchen when he heard his name. "It's in Russia, the amulet, it's in Russia."

"I don't think so Famous, the first one was in   Russia."

"Okay, think about it, prayer, it's a monastery. Innocence begins, you said it talked of a child. That has to be where my mom found me. A place of peace where no word is spoken, the temple, I don't think the monks speak in the temple. Finally, for one the past, will leave, but forgiveness will stay until the child returns. This is where it cinches it for me. The first amulet represents the past it must have left there with my mom. The last amulet must represent forgiveness, which stayed. I have to go to Russia, I'm the child that must return."

Jonathon sat there for a minute, knowing she must be right. All of the clues fit, "Daniel, can you take her to the Dublin airport? I'll book your flight. Well, while you're in Russia, I guess I need to figure out what Famous has to do with those amulets when she gets back."

Daniel nodded, "Maybe I should go with her."

"No," Famous looked at them, "This is my journey!" She ran up the stairs and grabbed her bag. Shoving her mother's journal back in the Ziploc. She ran back down the stairs and went into the kitchen to talk to Ellie. "Ellie, I know I can trust you more than anyone else in the world." She handed her the six amulets, "Hide them in a safe place and tell no one that you have them." Ellie nodded and shoved them in her apron pocket.

Daniel was waiting for her in the bean bag room with Jonathon, "Are you ready Daniel?" He nodded his head. "Jonathon, just message me the plane confirmation number." With that they were out the door.

Jonathon had looked up the flight, there were several, he booked the flight that departed in less than six hours. The drive took a couple of hours and he knew she would have to be there at least two hours before the flight. He couldn't help but hope she was right. It seemed to fit, but if she was wrong. Would it be another twenty plus years or even another hundred? He pushed the thought from his head and texted her the confirmation.

CHAPTER THIRTY FOUR

A PLACE OF PEACE

They had driven for nearly an hour when Daniel hit something and the tire exploded. Luckily he had a spare, but his jack wasn't working very well. Daniel kept trying with very little luck. A man in a truck stopped and offered assistance. His jack was in perfect working order. It didn't take long after that to be back on the road. They thanked him and were on their way. Famous looked at the time, they had lost nearly an hour.

Daniel drove a little faster, but knew they didn't have the time to get pulled over in one of the small towns along the way. She said good bye before they had even came to a complete stop in front of departures. Famous sprung from the car and ran to check in. The line moved quickly, she had her boarding pass in minutes.

For the second day in a row she was going through airport security. The line was very long, she kept looking at the time. Thinking it was going to be close. The man in front of her got stopped for an inspection of his luggage. It slowed her down even more, she hoped they didn't flag her too or that may be the nail in her coffin. She reached the gate as they were doing the final boarding call.

Famous shoved her backpack under the seat in front of her, sat back, and exhaled. She was thinking, I made it, as she fastened her seatbelt. The flight attendants went through their normal checklists. She was trying to remember the last time she was on a plane. It must have been the trip to Mexico. That made her think of her mother's letters. She laid back for takeoff and closed her eyes.

Famous must have fallen asleep because when she opened her eyes they were preparing for landing. She took a bus to the train station and the night train toward the ice caves. When she reached the small town she tried to ask for directions to the monastery. She didn't have much luck finding someone who understood English. Part of her believed they did, but were secretive about the monastery. She found a few tourist brochures for the ice caves. They were in Russian on one side and English on the other.

She made her way to the tourist office, she didn't have the time to hike it. The next tour would be leaving soon so she bought a ticket and waited. She looked around at the snow and the quaint town, it was beautiful. She was reminded of a Christmas movie. Her and her mother would watch them every night of December for as long as she could remember.

There were several trips up to the ice caves. You could stay and catch any of the return trips during business hours. She looked at the time and knew she would have only a few hours. She had to be on one of the return trips. When they reached the ice caves she walked around looking at the landscape. On any other day, if she were any other tourist, she would have missed the strange snow covered formation in a crevice of the mountain. She separated herself from the group and waited until the coast was clear.

Hiking in the snow was brutal, she was shivering and had fallen several times. She slid off a rock and hit her shoulder. Her heart was thumping, she was thinking of how close she was to hitting her head. There was a crunching in the snow just past the trees. She scrambled back to her feet and looked for a place to hide. She looked in front of her and then behind. She saw her track in the snow leading to right where she stood. There was no way to hide that. She started to make tracks going in different directions, but no matter where she stopped so did the tracks.

Famous stood still listening, the sound had stopped. She exhaled loudly, "Hello", a voice startled her from behind. She jumped and turned around. She felt the pounding in her chest through all of her body. She was shaking, "I'm so sorry, I didn't mean to startle you. Are you lost?"

Famous stood there staring, speechless for several seconds. "I, um, no, I was looking for you. Well not just you, the monastery. You see I am Famous."

He was a young monk, and the way he was looking at her she thought maybe he knew nothing of her. "Famous, you are Famous?" He looked at her incredulously. "Really, Famous, Famous, like the baby Famous. I thought it was all a tall tale." He put his hand on her shoulder. She winced and pulled away. "Are you hurt?"

"I fell," her adrenalin had been pumping so hard she hadn't noticed the pain until that very second. Tears welled up in her eyes.

"Follow me, I'm Brother Sam, are you okay to walk?" She nodded, "Okay, wow, Famous, follow me." She followed behind him, stepping in his tracks. It was a long trek, they circled around the trees and walked up an incline to a big wooden door. She looked around and realized she was heading the wrong way to the right place. From this advantage she could see that she never would have made it.

He rang the bell and opened the door. It was cozy inside, she could smell the fire. She wondered how it was that she didn't see any smoke outside from the fire. Slowly several monks entered the room. An elder looked dismayed at her presence. "Brother Sam, would you care to explain?"

The young monk looked like he was ready to explode. "She's Famous, you know, Dar's Famous. You know… the whole prophecy."

The elder held up his hand as if to tell him to be quiet. He walked to her, "Yes, I know Brother Sam, I know all too well. He looked in her eyes, "Famous?"

She spoke softly, "Yes, I am famous." He put his arm around her shoulder to usher her to warm by the fire. "Careful," she pulled her shoulder away. The young monk had said that she was hurt. The elder removed her coat and backpack. Her arm was bruised and swollen. He led her to a chair near the fire. "I have so much running through my mind? I have so many questions, but I am so limited on time. My mother…I"

He interrupted her, "I was sorry to hear of your mother's passing, she was such a magical person. We don't usually pay attention to the outside world, but we enjoyed the letters she sent us every month. I'm sorry, I'm Brother Davis, perhaps she mentioned me." Famous started thinking how all these years she was writing to so many people and she had had no idea. When did she find the time?

"I need to take a look at that shoulder." He placed a hot cloth on her shoulder. "It looks like it is dislocated." He called for the young monk to come back in the room. "We have to reset her shoulder." He gave him instructions, "This is not going to feel great, Famous. Brace yourself on the count of three," he grabbed her arm and pulled hard on her count of two. She felt it pop, screamed in pain, and pulled her arm against her chest. "Brother we will need a sling."

Tears were burning her cheeks, she wiped her eyes. The monk came back and held her hair while the elder tied the sling behind her neck. "I had almost given up hope that you were coming. We've been expecting you for years. Why did it take you so long?"

She shook her head, "I don't know, I think in a way I buried myself when I buried her. So this is where it all began?"

He smiled, "I guess you could say that. I found your mother and she found you."

"Where was I and how did she find me?"

He got up and walked around the room, "It's an unbelievable story really. You were left here in front of the door in a basket. She rang the bell, I only caught a glimpse of her and then she was gone. Like she disappeared, I can't explain it. There was a note saying you were of great importance. Your birth certificate was with the note, here's where it gets unbelievable. Your mother's name was already on it."

"How is that possible?"

"I said it was unbelievable, didn't I? Anyway the note went on to say your mother would come to find you soon. I think it's all connected somehow."

"I might find the answer if you could help me out with something." Famous told him the story of the amulets and the final clues. She gave him the paper with all of the clues on it. "Will you look in the temple, it must be there?"

"A place of peace, I think I might know where it is, but it's not in the temple. Follow me." Famous groaned as she stood up. "You poor dear, I can go look."

"No, I'm okay," she followed him into the temple. Famous was in awe of its magnificence. They walked to the front there were candles and a pedestal at the base of the stairs. He continued past and around to a side door. He put his finger to his lips and motioned her inside. There were a few monks inside. They began looking around, she opened her mouth, but he shook his head.

Famous noticed a mural painted on the wall it was a beautiful scenery, a calm lake with trees. On the bottom was the artist's name, E. Peace. She pointed at it. They both got really close, Famous ran her fingers across the letters. She motioned for something to pry into the wall. He shrugged and put up his finger as if to say he'd be right back.

He ran out the door and within minutes he reappeared with a letter opener. She scratched at the wall, the monk could see she was struggling using her left hand. He took the letter opener and dug into the wall until the metal amulet was visible. It took several minutes for them to free it. He placed it in her hand and smiled.

They walked out into the hall and he closed the door. "That is where the vow of silence is taken."

"Ah, it all makes sense now. I don't know how I can thank you enough." They walked back in and sat by the fire. "It's funny, you know?"

"What?"

"I started all of this because my mom wanted me to. Now I'm here and I still don't have the answers I thought I was looking for. But I was asking the wrong questions. I think I've found the answers that I needed, at least for now."

He smiled at her epiphany, "So where do you go from here?"

"Back to Ireland, I guess, maybe that's where I find the rest of those answers that I'm looking for. I need to get back to the ice caves before that last return trip. I so wish I had more time to spend here. Do you still have the note?"

He shook his head, "It was in the basket with you when your mom took you. I will have Brother Sam take you back to the ice caves, there is plenty of time."

CHAPTER THIRTY FIVE

CLUELESS

She felt a little sad leaving the monastery. Brother Sam led her back to the ice caves. "I hope no one notices I now have a sling on now when I didn't earlier." She smiled and waved as Brother Sam left her where the shuttle would be picking her up. A few others joined her as she waited. She just smiled at them as they walked up.

When she reached town she found a small restaurant that offered free Wi-Fi, she emailed Jonathon she was on her way back to the airport, if he could get her a flight back to Dublin. She got a ticket on the next train. She sat back on the train and closed her eyes for a minute. She knew she needed to read further in her mom's journal. She opened the journal and continued where she had left off.

Brother Davis left the room and came back with a large basket. He set it down next to me, she was so beautiful. I couldn't believe the note and birth certificate. She was the reason I was put on this earth. In my heart

I know this to be true. I picked her up and held her. I looked into her tiny baby face and said, I will call you Famous.

In the basket was a note, a birth certificate, and a small amulet with some letters and strange pictures on it. I asked Brother Davis about it, he said he was once told a fable. Seven such amulets and a child would right a wrong from years that were long gone. He said that there was a book about the amulets, but he knew no more. Brother Davis arranged for me to go to the hospital.

I had to have my leg put in a cast which made traveling with a baby back to Ireland a real challenge. Ellie came to Dublin personally to pick us up from the airport. I went back to the castle a couple of days later, I took Famous with me. After the normal tea drinking, Angelica appeared, she looked at Famous and whispered that she was to be her savior. She asked if we had brought the seven amulets. I could see her disappointment when I said I only had one, but not with me. I told her I didn't know where the other six were.

I found myself on the door step with Famous. The thought scared me to near death. I thought to myself, what if, what if she had kept Famous?

Famous was tired, her shoulder ached, and now she was nervous about going back. She thought back to the day she had met the witch. She knew her, all about her, she said. She seemed angry and now Famous understood why. She laid down on the seats using her backpack as a pillow. She must have slept through several stops when she woke she was nearly at her stop.

It had been a long twenty four hours and she felt like she could sleep for days. She boarded a bus for the airport. When Famous got to the airport she was able to check her email and found a confirmation for her flight from Jonathon. He said Daniel offered to pick her up since he was already in Dublin.

Security was very busy at this time in the evening. She stood in line for an hour. When she finally got through security, she was lucky to get to the gate before they started boarding. Her plane ride seemed like an eternity, she dozed off and on. Famous tried to get her mother's journal out of her head. It was no use, she reached into her bag and pulled it out. She flipped to the next page.

I haven't written in weeks, I am feeling so much sadness for Angelica. I have stayed on for nearly a month and we have come no closer to finding the book or the other amulets. Ellie and Edmond have been lovely and would allow me to stay for as long as I would like. I got word today that my mother has taken ill so I must return home. I don't know my future, but I must concern myself with the future of Famous and my mother. I can't continue with the past any longer. The minute Jonathon finds an answer I will come back. I hope it's soon, she's suffered long enough.

Famous sat there thinking how horrible it must have been for her to have to leave. Jonathon had said he had spent years on this with no resolve until the day he met Daniel. So much time had passed, Angelica had probably given up and then Famous appeared in her entryway. Famous was grateful when the plane landed, she needed to rest. Daniel was waiting outside for her. "What did you do to your arm?"

"Long story," she set her backpack in front of her as she climbed in the car. Daniel closed her door for her, he asked her if she had found the last one. "Yes, it was there and I have it, so I hope this will all be over soon."

"I'd like to see them, all seven of them together." There was something about his voice that put her on edge. "Show them to me!" He sounded like he was demanding to see them. She was probably just tired.

"Okay, when we get to Ellie's. I don't have them all with me, just the one from Russia. I certainly didn't want to lose them. Could you imagine going through all of that, I couldn't take the risk." He drove toward Ellie's, it was a couple hours from Dublin. They were near Ellie's house, she watched as he passed her road, "You missed the turn."

"I want to show you something."

"I'm really tired, can you show me tomorrow. I'd really like to just lie down for a while." He kept driving, "Daniel I really want to go to Ellie's, please turn around." He didn't respond to her, she reached in her purse for her phone, he knocked it out of her hand. "What is going on, Daniel?"

"I told you, I'm going to show you something." The tone in his voice made her nervous. Her arm was useless, she couldn't reach for the door handle even if he did come to a stop. They approached an old stone house, he pulled up and turned off the engine. She tried to grab the door with her other hand, but she was struggling with the seatbelt. Daniel opened her door and pulled her out of the car. She cried out in pain when he grabbed her arm.

"I really don't understand what is going on, where are we?" She looked around, but it was dark, there were no lights. He grabbed her arm again and she pulled away from him. "You need to stop this, my arm is hurt." She grabbed her backpack and was about to run when he grabbed her backpack and ripped it from her hand. "That's mine," she reached for it, but he started walking toward the cottage.

"C'mon," he growled at her. She could hear her phone ringing on the floorboard of his car.

She turned and ran for it before he realized it she was answering it. "Jonathon, it's Daniel, he's…" He smashed her phone on the ground. She knew Jonathon would be concerned with the way she screamed in the phone.

"I said c'mon," he grabbed her arm again. The pain seared through her, she turned and kicked him as hard as she possibly could. He let go long enough for her to grab the backpack and start running. He chased her and caught up to her and dragged her back to the cottage. Daniel put her in a wooden chair and tied her legs to the chair legs. He tied her torso to the chair back. He paced back and forth for a while. "You were supposed to have them with you. This was supposed to be easy, do you have any idea how long my family has looked for those amulets?"

She watched him walk back and forth, yelling about the amulets. Most of what he said didn't make sense to her, but she was starting to put the pieces together. "Is that why you stole the book and took the copies to Jonathon?"

"They belong to me, you have no right to them!" He snarled at her, "And you're going to get them for me."

"Oh no I'm not, I have a destiny to fulfil. This is something I have to do."

"It's always been this way, your family against mine." Famous was confused, she listened to his rant. What could he possibly know about her family? She had a mother and grandmother, both deceased. "You don't get it do you? That witch that put that curse was my great, great, great, well, I don't know how many greats, but grandmother. The white witches stole the amulets and separated them. Which killed my grandmother."

"I don't understand what does all of this have to do with me?"

He walked up to her and looked in her eyes, "I can't believe you don't know, I think you're playing stupid." She was trying to put the pieces together, but she was scared and her arm was throbbing.

"I will give you the amulets after I set Angelica free."

"Seriously, you are clueless."

"Why are you being so mean, I just offered them to you. I've done nothing to you." She felt tears in her eyes, but she wasn't breaking down. Her fear turned to anger. She was getting more and more angry, and started to try to wriggle out of the ropes. Every movement sent pain through her whole body. "So if I'm so clueless, enlighten me, Daniel. If you're so smart spell it out for me!"

"If the seven amulets are used to break one of her spells now that she's dead it will render them useless. I can't allow that to happen. Together they hold so much power and that power belongs to me."

"Okay fine, first of all, I'm not stupid. I didn't know any of this. Second, other than the fact I was trying to free Angelica, what does it have to do with me."

"Only you can break the spell. Your mother died when she was separating the amulets. The white witches that stole the amulets, that's why two of the amulets ended up in the same location. The monastery, it's all in the book. Your grandmother took you there after your mother died, but it didn't give the location. The missing pages in the book were about me. I took the pages about descendants out before I gave it to Professor Dowel.

I had to steal the original book. I cast a spell on the book and the copies so they would always return to me. I had no idea Jonathon had written down the clues to the amulets. The other thing I didn't know was that he knew your mother. The one that raised you, not your birth mother."

Famous sat there in shock for a few minutes. So she was a witch too? He looked at her and could tell this was all new information. He shook his head, "I can't believe you didn't know."

"Well, how could I have known? You're awfully judgmental, and just so you know I will never give them to you!"

"I'll trade you for them, or maybe I'll just go get them. I'll figure it out by the morning." He sat down on the couch and leaned back.

Famous started to look around for the first time. She noticed, dried herbs, strange bottles of liquids, and jars of odd looking things. She was in the witch's house. This sudden realization made her angrier. How dare he bring her here? "Are you serious? You are just going to leave me tied up here all night?"

"That's the plan," Daniel looked like he was dozing off, his head bobbed a few times. She looked around again trying to find a way to free herself. If she were a witch wouldn't she have powers, or maybe it doesn't work like that. How would she know, not even her own mother knew. At least she didn't think so.

She had to find a way to get out of here. She wiggled and wiggled, all it did was hurt. She tried to scrunch her shoulders together. That was absolute agony, but she kept trying. The rope felt like it was cutting into her arms. There must be something she could do. Daniel started to move a little, she closed her eyes and slumped her head forward to look like she was asleep. A few minutes went by, she heard him snore a little. She slowly looked up, he was asleep.

Famous looked around the room, there's got to be something. She said it over and over. She closed her eyes and tried to think of a way out of the ropes. The amulet in her pocket felt warm. She wondered, what could it mean? They have power, but she was thinking you had to have all seven, but maybe that was just to break the spell. She closed her eyes again and visualized the ropes falling off her. It got warmer and warmer. She thought the ropes were feeling looser. Yes they were looser, she kept at it until she could bare the heat burning her leg no more. She opened her eyes and wiggled a little, but Daniel moved, she looked at him again and again. She held her breath and didn't move every time she thought he might be waking up.

One of the ropes slid down, she tried to pull her shoulders into her chest. The pain was nearly unbearable, but she kept on. Another rope slipped down to her waist this time. She had to sit back and take a deep breath. Tears were streaming down her face, but she was not giving up. She stared at the ropes and again the amulet began to get warm again. Famous felt like she used every ounce of her energy but the ropes fell and her arms were freed.

She had only her left hand to untie her feet, she kept looking up at Daniel. Once her feet were untied, she gently picked up her backpack and crept toward the door. She was suddenly grateful for stone floors. But the door, it seemed like every door in Ireland creaked loudly when it was opened. She knew she couldn't outrun him. Famous wandered around looking for another exit. She saw a window she might be able to squeeze out. Why did they make them so small back then? With her shoulder, she would never make it out before he woke up.

There was only one way out, so what was she waiting for? She turned the knob slowly, her eyes on Daniel the whole time. Opening the door an inch at a time, she just needed it open enough to squeeze out. Daniel moved a little, she stared at him, thinking he had better not dare move off that couch. His eyes opened, but he didn't budge. Their eyes were locked, he looked like he was trying to get up. It was her holding him there, but her concentration was broken.

She ran out into the night. Famous used the cover of darkness. Famous thought that she just had to put enough distance between them. There were no other houses for miles. She calculated they were going about thirty miles per hour between Ellie's and here. It took about ten minutes, calculated, and trying to run quietly. She must be about five miles from Ellie's. Now that she just ran for ten minutes she wasn't sure what direction to go.

She crouched down in a field when she saw headlights. That's how they always get caught in those scary movies. They run out thinking they'll be saved and it's the bad guy. Well, not her, the car passed. She couldn't tell if it was Daniel or not, but she wasn't taking any chances. It was hard to crawl across the wet grass with one arm and a backpack. Her legs were soaked from the knees down and she was having to drag her backpack. She didn't care, she had to get as far away as possible.

Famous stopped for a minute to listen for any sound that he was behind her. She knew she had made it past the dim light from the house before he got outside. She had that going for her. He didn't know what direction she went. A sudden thought, neither did she.

That didn't matter now. All that mattered is that she could not allow Daniel to get those seven amulets. He could possibly get the other six. As long as he didn't have her, he would never have the seventh. Six would be bad, but all seven, she couldn't even imagine what he could do.

She heard nothing, slowly she got to her feet. Famous glanced around hoping she would see something, anything that would help her with direction. It was so dark and the field was nearly as tall as she was. This was good and bad for her, she didn't know if she should be grateful or not.

Famous thought about her compass, she was trying to replay what direction they had gone from Ellie's. She was in such shock he had passed their road. Think Famous, think, she closed her eyes trying for the life of her to picture it. The compass only helps if you know the direction you want to go.

Famous pulled the amulet out of her pocket. This amulet represents forgiveness, but she felt like it helped her before. It didn't make sense, maybe it didn't help her. She started thinking of how hot it had gotten. Maybe it hindered her, it was about this time she wished she had learned more about witchcraft. She had read books on it in the library, but none of them said anything about stuff like this. She continued walking in some unknown direction. She hid again when she saw another set of headlights.

She knew she could make it in an hour or two to Ellie's, if she could just figure out which way to go. She walked through the field until she came to a road. She looked through the grass to see if there were any signs. She didn't want to come out of the cover of the field. She vaguely remembered them taking a right and a left a ways after Ellie's and they drove down a long road. It was all she had so she turned right and followed the road far enough in to be hidden by the grass.

She couldn't even tell how long she had been walking. Technology, her phone, was how she kept track of time. She knew it felt like an eternity. She came to a road where she had to turn left or right. Logic told her if she went right she would go back the way she came so she was going to go left. She was either going closer to Ellie's or even farther away. She looked in all directions before coming out of the safety of the field. Famous darted across the street, unfortunately the field on that side had been freshly mowed.

Famous was willing to take her chances, if she saw any lights she'd lay down if she had to.

She got lucky, the next property down had several trees lining the road. It had to have been an hour, she thought, anytime now she'd be recognizing something. If not she would have to believe she was going the wrong way. About that moment when her guard was down a car came over the hill. She stood still hoping the trees would give her cover. Surely if she tried to run behind a tree the movement might catch the driver's eye. The car was moving really slow.

CHAPTER THIRTY SIX

WHERE DO WE GO FROM HERE?

Famous stood holding her breath hoping against all hope the lights would not hit her directly. The lights did just that and the car came to a stop. Famous couldn't make out the car and started to bolt when she heard Ellie's voice, "Famous is that you? We have been searching for you for hours."

Famous ran to her, her eyes were full of tears, "I can't tell you how happy I am to see you. How did you know I wasn't still in Dublin?"

"That was Jonathon, get in the car and I'll tell you all about it." Famous climbed in the car and sat back with a sigh of relief. She knew it wasn't over, but for one second she just wanted to breathe. "Jonathon was able to make some calls and find out the cell tower where your phone last pinged when you answered his call. We have been driving the whole grid looking for you. What in the world happened?"

"It's Daniel, he is a descendant of the witch that cast the spell and he wants the amulets. It gets even crazier too." She began telling them the story. She had barely scratched the surface of the story when they pulled up to Ellie's. "You did put those amulets in a safe place right Ellie?"

"Of course, they are locked up tight."

"I have a feeling we haven't seen the last of Daniel." Famous looked all around before she got out of the car. Jonathon went in front of Ellie after she unlocked the door.

"Did Daniel do that to your arm?"

Famous shook her head, "Nope that was all me, he certainly didn't help matters after the fact though. I dislocated when I was trying to climb up to the monastery." She shut the door behind her and slide the large bolt across for extra security. "I have so much more to tell you, you are never going to guess who my birth mother was."

Ellie and Jonathon were standing there waiting for an answer when Edmond came down. "Famous, thank God, you are okay. Are you hungry? Would you like some hot cocoa?"

"Yes and yes, but first I have to get out of these wet clothes. Same room?" She pointed at the stairs. Ellie nodded and followed Edmond into the kitchen to give him a hand. She filled him in on what she knew so far. Famous came down, "Um, Ellie, can you possibly give me a hand." Ellie climbed the stairs, Famous handed her the top to her fuzzy pajamas.

"We're in here," Edmond yelled from the bean bag room. Famous and Ellie went in and snuggled down by the fire. Famous was exhausted, but had so much to tell them.

"Jonathon, if I am correct, Daniel is going to show up tomorrow at Angelica's. What happens with him and the seven amulets all in one place at one time?"

"First things first, start at the beginning, Russia, and then tell us everything. We are totally in the dark other than knowing Daniel basically kidnapped you." Famous began her story from the time she landed in Russia. She detailed every moment, they almost felt like they were in the room with her. Hours had passed and she felt like she had given them every detail. Famous continued to snack all the way through.

"So, now that you know everything, where do we go from here?"

Jonathon looked at her, "Forward, tomorrow we will move forward. We will go to Angelica's with the seven amulets and you will free her. Luckily, he was genuinely shocked that I was here. He didn't know me at all, when he brought me the copies of the book. Therefore, most of the book is there including how to do exactly that, free Angelica.

It seems like he only took out facts of her having descendants. I copied most of the pages I felt were important before you two woke up the other day. Knowing it could disappear, when Daniel left. I'll study it and hopefully have more answers for you in the morning. Right now you should definitely get some rest."

Ellie patted her leg, "You're going to need it."

CHAPTER THIRTY SEVEN

THE LIGHT

The morning seemed like it came before she even laid down. She didn't even want to open her eyes. She ached everywhere, when she sat up her whole upper torso could barely move. She stepped into the shower and looked down at the bruises on her knees. She couldn't lift her right arm to wash her hair. Her left arm was so tired from the previous night. She was battered, but not beaten. This was what she was born for. Her whole life led to this day. This is who she is, that thought was everything her mom wanted for her.

She was the strong-willed, kind, part her mother, she guessed part her birth mother, and incredibly a witch. She found herself as her mom found her. Maybe she even found more of herself. The water was hot, she needed the relaxing feel of the hot water rushing over her aching body. She stepped out of the shower when she heard Ellie at the door. Famous put on a bath robe and yelled for her to come in.

"Good morning, Ellie, how did you sleep?"

"Okay, I guess, it's been like 'déjà vu' like I've been here before. I remember when your mom was here. It was heart wrenching when you two left, I'm not saying it wasn't the right thing to do. She needed to be with your grandmother and she gave it a real effort. Without that book, well, you know. So are you ready for this?"

"I don't know, if it weren't for Daniel, I'd say definitely, but he's like a wild card that I didn't count on. I just don't really know what I am doing or even what to expect. I do feel like he is going to cause a problem."

"Oh, we can be sure of that." Famous was overwhelmed, it was supposed to be over years ago. Her birthmother died and the book was lost. Her grandmother improvised. How did she know her mother? Because the book was lost, the location of the amulets died with her. "The reason I came up is Jonathon wants to talk to you."

"Okay, tell him I'll be right down after I get dressed." Getting dressed took longer than anticipated. Famous slowly walked down the stairs. She felt a stabbing pain with every step. When she reached the bottom Ellie handed her a cup of coffee, "Thank you, I really need this."

She walked into the beanbag room, Jonathon had papers strewn about the floor.

"We have a problem," he looked like he hadn't slept. "If Daniel shows up at Angelica's while you're there with the seven amulets. If he gets ahold of them he can banish you to the same fate as Angelica."

"He is not going to get ahold of them."

"The problem is even though you have them you are so weak compared to him. You know nothing about spells or curses, he's lived this his whole life. I wished I had known. I'm afraid this is going to be too dangerous for you."

"Do I have a choice?" Famous sipped on her coffee, "I mean, what other options, do I have? I have to break this curse or spell or whatever. The amulets will then be useless, Angelica will be free, and I will have some closure to this chapter in my life. Not only for me, but also for my mom."

"Even if it means it can kill you?"

Ellie walked in as Jonathon asked Famous. "Kill her, what are you talking about?"

"I have to be honest, Ellie, I just don't think she is strong or knowledgeable enough for this fight. Just take a look at her," he pointed at Famous. "Not only has she been injured, but she's not ready to take this on."

Famous walked back and forth for a few minutes. "Well you better get me ready and quick!"

"Are you sure?"

Famous exhaled, "I'm afraid so."

Ellie looked outside, she was jittery about Daniel. She had worried all night about him lurking about. She knew they were safe as long as they were safely locked inside, but all bets were off the second Famous walked outside with those amulets. Jonathon began explaining to Famous what she had to do. He explained everything in detail. It wasn't particularly difficult as long as Daniel didn't show up. Jonathon had a plan, but it all hinged on getting Famous into Angelica's castle without being seen. Which would be next to impossible.

"Let's do this," Famous asked Ellie for the amulets. "I am just going to go over and get it done and over with. The whole thing looks like it will take five minutes."

"Famous, as long as the amulets are in your hands you'll be safe. The second you put them down around Angelica you will be vulnerable. So we are going to do everything in our power to keep Daniel out. The realtor will be there at nine so we need to go. Ellie maybe you should wait here."

"I'm going, period, I know you and Edmond are going to do everything in your power to protect Famous. I can't just sit here wondering and waiting."

"Fine, you go in with Famous, Edmond and I will guard the door. Let's go."

Ellie had gone to get the amulets. Famous had the last one in her pocket. She was looking at the drawing Jonathon had given her. Each one had to be placed in the correct order. That was going to be the challenging part, they all looked so similar. "Hey Jonathon, I think I should put them in order now."

"Good idea," Ellie walked in and handed them to Famous. There was a banging on the door. Ellie looked out, but couldn't see anyone, she started to slide the lock when Famous grabbed her hand and shook her head. The door started to shake and it was a big heavy door.

Famous looked at Ellie, "Is there another way out?"

"Famous, it doesn't matter, he cannot touch you as long as you have all seven of the amulets. He can follow you, terrorize you, and whatever, to try to get you to lose control of them. You must remember that, the time of concern is when you have to place them around Angelica. You don't exactly have seven hands."

The door continued to rattle, "I don't want to go out there with that going on."

"That's what he's counting on. He wants to distract you as long as possible. Now put those things in order and let's go. I wrote what you need to say on the back."

Famous read it, "Are you sure? I was kind of expected something more antiquated or, I don't know, just more!"

"Just trust me, it has to include the amulets in the order of placement. Famous, we went over all of this."

"I know, I know, I'm a little nervous. Let's just get this over with." Jonathon motioned Ellie to open the door. Famous looked out, but Daniel wasn't there. They all walked out and climbed into the car. Famous closed the door, but it flew open again. She grabbed the handle and pulled it closed and locked it. It completely flew off. "How can he be this powerful?" She could feel heat radiating from the amulets.

"He's trying to get control of those amulets, he is summoning them. Famous you have to maintain control." Jonathon started the car, Famous closed her eyes and blocked out the rest of the world. It was only a short distance away, she told herself over and over. But it felt like the longest half mile of her life. The realtor was standing in front of the door. At least they thought she was a realtor.

Famous walked toward the door, the woman was older than she would have expected. "Famous?"

Famous looked at her, although she didn't know her there was something so familiar about her. She stared at her for a second, "Yes, I..." she stopped in mid-sentence. "Do I know you?"

The door creaked open, it startled Famous. "You first Famous," she smiled, Famous couldn't shake the feeling that she should know who this woman is. Famous walked in, but didn't see Angelica at first.

Crazy things were happening, it was raining inside, and objects were flying about the room. "So you've come back, Famous." Angelica stood there in the form of a witch. The darkness and chaos were distracting to Famous. The other woman gently touched Famous on the shoulder. It was unlike anything she had ever felt before. Her touch made Famous feel warmth and a light radiated around her.

Daniel appeared in the doorway. "Go ahead Famous put them down." He taunted her, thunder roared, lightning flashed. She could see him in the flashes of light.

"I'm here to help protect you." The woman said.

Famous closed her eyes to gather her strength. She took several deep breaths, blocking out all of the negativity. Surrounding herself by the brightest light, Daniel had to shield his eyes. Ellie, Edmond, and Jonathon had tried to go in, but couldn't make it past the threshold. They could see nothing, but light. A light too bright to see past.

Famous walked to Angelica, she had strength like she had never known. She kneeled at Angelicas feet. "From the **past**," she laid down the amulet that represented the past. "With <u>love </u>and <u>purity</u>," she continued with each amulet as she said the words. "I ask for the <u>safety </u>of the white light and for <u>forgiveness</u> to free this spirit from this <u>present </u>day. I ask the white light give her peace for all of <u>eternity</u>." She laid down the last amulet.

The room was filled with light brighter than any light Famous had ever seen. The beautiful princess Angelica smiled at Famous. "Thank you," She began to fade, "Your mother is so proud of you Famous." The light began to dissipate, it seemed like the whole world had been frozen in time.

Famous sat there on the floor for several minutes. She looked up at the woman, "You're my grandmother, aren't you? You sacrificed everything for this one moment. I'm not totally sure I understand why."

She smiled, "You do in your heart dear little Famous. You have ended this wickedness, but it's only your beginning."

EPILOGUE

Famous knew that she could never go back to the life she had had. There were letters to read and journals to explore. Adventures her mother had left for her. Adventures to come with a family she had never known. A destiny of righting the wrongs between good and bad witches. Two separate worlds with her as the only connection. She had found her path in life, but where would it take her?